THE NAUGHTY NEIGHBOR COLLECTION

BY

AVERY ROWAN

The Naughty Neighbor Collection

By Avery Rowan

First Edition

Copyright © 2019 Avery Rowan

All Rights Reserved

This book is a work of fiction. All names, characters, locations, and incidents are strictly products of the author's imagination. Any resemblance to actual persons, living or dead, is entirely coincidental.

This book is licensed for your personal enjoyment only and may not be reproduced in any form, except in assisting in a review. This book may not be resold. Thank you for respecting the hard work of this author.

For up-to-date news on Avery's latest releases, book signing events in your area, and giveaways, follow Avery's newsletter - http://eepurl.com/dCBBwP

BEING NEIGHBORLY

ONE

"C'mon, Linds," Brandon said, almost pleading. "We have the whole house to ourselves. A little skinny dip in the pool will keep us from being bored." He stared at her blond head as she sat in the recliner, one leg draped over the arm as she thumbed through one of his parents' magazines. Luckily, they were out for the weekend, giving Lindsey and him the entire house to themselves. However, he had yet to get Lindsey to make the most of their good fortune, and was getting tired of sounding like a whiny kid. "It's a beautiful day outside. We should go enjoy it."

Lindsey rolled her eyes. "Brandon, getting naked in the pool with you making excuses to try and grope me the entire time is not really my idea of a relaxing afternoon."

He sighed. "Linds, I'm sure we can make it a little more imaginative than that. Why not enjoy this time alone before my parents return home? We could be having sex all over this place."

Lindsey slammed her magazine closed and dropped her arms to her lap. "No. Forget it. What you mean is that you'll be getting off all over this house while leaving me unsatisfied and horny. I never realized that while you were in high school, all you ever did was jack off. I thought you had some inkling on how to satisfy a woman. Well, I'm not going to just lay there and take it, while you get what you want and I'm left yearning for my vibrator. No, thank you." She snapped the magazine open again and started reading, essentially blowing him off, and not in the way he wanted. "Besides, we never know when you're parents will pop back in, even when they're supposed to be gone for days. No. I don't need your mom catching us with our pants down again."

He stared at her a moment, hoping she would change her mind, but then he just gave up and left her alone. This was not how he expected married life to be. Lindsey had been so horny when they were first married, always wanting to fuck at the drop of a hat. Or their pants as the case may be. Yet, lately, she had just grown bored with it all and wouldn't tell him why.

With a sigh, he shoved himself off the couch and left her sitting there. He'd enjoy the beautiful day outside by himself. There was just no pleasing Lindsey when she was like this.

When he stepped outside, he noticed Meredith Walker heading back to her house from getting her mail. The forty-year-old woman had been an object of Brandon's fantasies since he first learned how good jacking off felt. She had long blond hair and the biggest breasts Brandon remembered seeing with a perfect ass that she showed off with the tight pants and skirts she wore. His father always watched her whenever he was working outside, and Brandon couldn't help but do the same. Meredith oozed sensuality that kept his twenty-year-old cock stiff and his dreams wet. If only Lindsey exuded the same sexiness. She used to, back when they first got married, even when they dated. However, lately, nothing seemed to get her juices wet.

Meredith glanced up after sorting through her mail and saw Brandon standing there staring at her. He waved, suddenly feeling as if had been busted in his naughty thoughts. Meredith just smiled, however, and waved back as she changed directions and headed his way. He tried hard not to stare at her hips or tits as they swayed with her movement across the grass but it was hard and he had to do a little chant in his head. *Stare at her eyes. Stare at her eyes.* He felt his breathing grow heavy and shoved a hand in his front pocket hoping to hide the growing erection he felt happening.

"Hey, Brandon," she said with a smile. "Enjoying the empty house?" Her smile turned to a mischievous grin. "When I was your age, I'd relish the time my parents left me alone in the empty house with someone of the opposite sex."

He sighed at the reminder that he wasn't having the kind of fun he had expected to be getting when his parents said they were leaving town for the weekend. "It's been kind of quiet."

She cocked her head to the side as she stared at him with narrowed eyes. "That didn't sound like a good kind of quiet. Everything okay?"

Brandon shrugged. "I kind of thought Lindsey would be relishing the empty house. We've been living here with my folks for six months without any time to ourselves. Sex hasn't exactly been a top priority. Of course, it hasn't been a top priority for her since they left, either." He shook his head. "I just don't get it."

"Well, maybe she's just tired," Meredith said. "Women tend to be more receptive in their own homes. Maybe she's just feeling a little off. Why don't you two come over to my house for dinner tonight? It'll be fun. We'll grill out, share some wine. How about seven?"

She didn't exactly make the offer seem like he could refuse, and besides, a night staring at Meredith's breasts would be a lot more fun being ignored by Lindsey all night. "Sounds good. Anything we can bring?"

Meredith grinned, her eyes twinkling at him as she said, "Just your appetite. See you tonight." She turned and walked away, her ass swaying with each step.

Brandon stood there staring at the older woman as she walked away, thinking that taking his appetite to her house later tonight would not be a problem. Of course, it wouldn't be his stomach he wanted to fill. With a deep breath, he forced himself to turn and walk away, adjusting his cock in his pants as he did. He was already looking forward to tonight.

TWO

"Why do we have to go over there again?" Lindsey sighed as she plopped down on the bed. "I just want to lay on the couch and watch TV."

"We do that every night," Brandon said as he pulled his shirt over his head. "Besides, Meredith has been a great friend of the family since we moved in here." *Not to mention how hot she looks in a bathing suit.* "It'll be fun. Promise."

She rolled her eyes, but still shoved herself off the bed. Walking over to Brandon, she ran a hand under his chin. "Don't think I'm stupid. I see how you and your father look at her when she's outside. I know how she affects you." She reached out and grabbed his cock through his jeans. "Right here."

He felt his eyes go wide as he shook his head. "I'll admit, she's a very pretty woman, but really, I don't look at her that way."

He pulled her close, wrapping an arm around her waist. "I only have eyes for you."

She gave a soft laugh. "You have eyes for anything with tits." She leaned up and kissed him on the cheek. "Okay, let's go get this evening over with so I can get back to my shows."

"You know, we can always entertain ourselves without the television." He squeezed her tighter against him. "I'm sure we can come up with something to keep us from getting bored."

She shook her head. "Let's just start with dinner, shall we? I wouldn't want to tax your imagination."

He sighed as she turned and walked out the bedroom door. He really wished he knew what had made her so uptight lately. With a deep breath, he followed her out the door and through the house.

Dusk had claimed the city by the time they knocked on Meredith's door, and Brandon was glad for the way the darkness hid his hard-on from where his mind had taken him the closer he got to his neighbor's front door. Lindsey was at least smiling, and had even seemed to be making the best of their evening, even though it wasn't what she wanted for their night. The visit at least got the two of them out of the house.

He turned to Lindsey, putting a reassuring smile on his face. "You ready?"

She smiled, and he couldn't tell if it was genuine or not. "Sure."

He took a deep breath, something he was getting used to doing, and knocked on the door. Only a couple of seconds passed before Meredith opened the door, greeting them. Brandon tried to control his gaze, but it was hard to do. Meredith had decided to wear a tight, low-cut top, which pushed her ample breasts up and over the top into plain view. She was also wearing a pair of tight jean shorts that cupped her ass, exposing the bottom curve of her ass cheeks. Brandon smiled as Meredith reached out and pulled him into a hug, her small hands pressing his back as her breasts pushed up into his face. She then reached over to Lindsey and pulled her into an equally tight embrace, only her hands went lower onto Lindsey's waist, just above her ass. Brandon watched as his wife smiled at the older woman, her eyes twinkling. Perhaps tonight would go better than Brandon expected.

"I'm glad you two could make it," Meredith said as she motioned for them to enter her home. "Thanks for keeping an old woman from being lonely."

"Old?" Lindsey said with a disbelieving tone. "Hardly. I hope I look as good as you do when I'm your age."

"That's sweet," Meredith said as she reached out and took Lindsey's hand, leading her to the kitchen.

Brandon watched as the two women walked ahead of him, still holding hands. He couldn't believe that Lindsey hadn't pulled her hand out of Meredith's after a couple of seconds. She wasn't much of a hand-holder. Yet, here she was, holding Meredith's hand as they walked and even leaning into the other woman as they whispered back and forth about women's beauty and age. Brandon just shook his head as he followed them, deciding it best to just go with it.

"So, Brandon, why don't you pour the wine, while I get the steaks off the grill?" Meredith instructed without releasing Lindsey's hand. "I'm going to drag your wife out with me to get to know her a little better. I can't believe you two have been married almost a year now."

Brandon stood in the middle of the kitchen and watched as the two women walked out the door, his beautiful wife and his neighbor, who had to be twice their age. However, both women looked hot as hell, their asses tight in their clothes and sashaying across the floor, almost as if both of them teased him. Brandon decided it was best to just untuck his shirt to cover the massive boner he sported. There was no way he could keep his hand in his pocket all night long to hide it. God, he hoped Lindsey was horny when they got back to the house. He was tired of waiting and going without.

Brandon took another deep breath as he walked over to the cabinet to get the wine glasses, wondering what would have happened if he had left Lindsey at home and came to dinner alone. He had been having fantasies of Meredith since he could remember, and he knew tonight there would be another one to add to his spank bank. He popped the cork on the wine bottle and the image only made him think of plunging his cock into Meredith's tight little cunt. He found himself gripping the wine bottle harder than necessary and, after a quick look to make sure the women weren't returning, he reached down and gripped his cock, moving his hard shaft in his pants, trying to find some relief.

None came, however.

THREE

All throughout dinner, Brandon kept one hand in his lap rubbing at his cock as he stared at the two gorgeous women on either side of him. Several glasses of wine were poured, and by the time they had left the kitchen and headed to the living room, everyone seemed to be feeling quite comfortable. Even Lindsey had come around and started smiling and even giggling. Brandon was shocked, considering how sour her mood had been the past few months.

When they entered the living room, Meredith took a seat on one end of the sofa, while pulling Lindsey down with her. Brandon took a seat in the recliner, not sure how crowded everyone wanted to be but wishing he was squished between the two ladies.

"Thank you both again," Meredith said as she settled back on the sofa, one hand holding her wineglass, the other draped over her knee. "It was sweet of you to join me for dinner, considering you had the entire house to yourselves. I'm sure you would have much rather been getting some snuggle time in with Brandon's parents gone."

A pained look came across Lindsey's face, and at first, Brandon thought she was going to say she was forced to come over but she didn't. Instead, she opened herself up to Meredith. "Actually, I'm glad we came over. Our nights haven't exactly been intimate. We seem to be stuck in some rut, and I'm sure it's just me tired of always having people around. I always wanted my own house so I could walk around in my undies if I wanted, you know."

Brandon squirmed in his seat, knowing he was to blame for Lindsey's unhappiness, but not sure what he could do about it. Money was what it was, and none of it was in abundance right now.

Meredith smiled as she reached over and patted Lindsey on the knee. "Oh, sweetie, I know exactly what you mean. There is nothing like the freedom of doing what you want in your own home, especially going around naked. To tell you the truth, I hate being clothed as well. So much freer when it's just your body, isn't it? And when you can look over and see your partner's nude body, their curves and all the special spots we love to touch and caress. Makes me squirm just thinking about it."

Lindsey nodded as she turned slightly so she was facing the other woman. Brandon just stared, never before seeing this intimate side of Meredith before. Sure, she was the neighbor next door he had pictured when he stroked himself off late at night under his covers, but to hear her talking like she was right then was just unreal. If she walked around naked all the time, he definitely should have visited more often.

"I agree," Lindsey said. "When I still lived with my parents, the minute they were out the door, I was out of my clothes and letting the air touch my body."

Meredith giggled, and it seemed so odd for a grown woman to laugh in such a way to Brandon. "You know what we should do?" she asked as she leaned closer to Lindsey as if whispering some dark secret of conspiracy. "We should just do it right now."

"Do what?" Brandon asked, afraid he already knew the answer. Or rather, hoping he knew the answer.

Lindsey's eyes went wide and her mouth popped open as if she wanted to say something, but Meredith grabbed her by the hand and pulled her to her feet. "Come on. Let's do it." Meredith said, and with a mischievous grin on her face, she reached for the hem of her shirt and pulled it up and over her head, dropping it to the floor at her feet. She then reached behind her and unclasped her bra, pulling it off her arms and tossing it to the floor with her shirt. Brandon just stared, wide-eyed, with his mouth partly open, at the most gorgeous set of round tits he had ever seen. Her nipples were small and pink and hard as ever, and he yearned to take them in his mouth and suck on them. "Well, come on Lindsey,"

Meredith said as she reached for the buttons on her shorts. "Don't leave me out here alone."

Brandon turned to his wife, expecting her to be angry and storm out of the house. However, instead, she reached for her shirt and pulled it off her body, dumping it on top of Meredith's, and then, she added her bra to the pile. The older woman had slowed down, waiting on Lindsey to catch up, but as soon as they were topless, they both unbuttoned their shorts, loosened them, yanked the zippers down, and then slid them down their legs along with their underwear.

Naked.

Both women stood there stark naked, asses firm and begging to be groped, breasts pushed out wanting to be suckled. Brandon could only sit there and stare, afraid that if he said a word, the moment would pass and both women would get dressed again. He did not want them to get dressed again. His cock throbbed within his pants, aching to be out and stroked, his breathing heavy in his ears. He didn't know what to do.

Then, both women turned to him, grinning. "I don't think it's fair that we're the only ones naked. Do you, Lindsey?" Meredith asked, gliding her tongue over her lips after she said it.

Lindsey put her hands on her waist, one hip jutting out a little in her cocky manner as she stared at him. Brandon squirmed under her gaze. Surely, she wouldn't go along with this? His luck couldn't be that good, could it? "No, Meredith, I don't. Seems a man would want to be as naked as us and not make us feel awkward." Then she bit her lower lip and grinned at him.

"Well, Brandon," Meredith said. "I think it's time for you to strip."

FOUR

Brandon stared at Meredith, not believing what she had just told him, had just commanded basically, for him to do. To add to his confusion, his wife, Lindsey, just stood there and waited for him to obey their host. His heart raced as he ran his tongue over his dry lips, contemplating the consequences if this was some test Lindsey was giving him.

"Well?" Lindsey asked, moving her arms over her chest. Her eyes glinted as she stared at him, and he saw a desire there he hadn't seen in a while.

"I think he's a little scared," Meredith said. "Perhaps, we should help motivate him." She then turned, grabbed Lindsey's arm, and swung his wife around to face her. Without hesitation, Meredith reached up, sliding a hand behind Lindsey's neck, and pulled the younger woman to her, kissing her full on the mouth, the open mouth. He could tell Meredith's tongue was probing his wife, saw Meredith's other hand glide down Lindsey's back to cup her ass, squeezing it as she pressed their bodies together. Lindsey moaned as she slid her arms around the older woman, embracing her as the kiss continued.

Brandon stared, his cock throbbing within his pants, begging to be released.

When the ladies broke the kiss, Meredith turned to face him, a pout on her face that he was still dressed. "I thought for sure you'd be naked when we finished. Brandon, that's not how a gentleman acts." She walked over to him, her pink nipples hardened buds that drew his eyes to them. When she reached him, she placed her hand on his chest, leaning in and whispering in his ear, "I want you naked, Brandon."

He took a long, slow, deep breath. He glanced over Meredith's shoulder at Lindsey, who was walking over to him as well. When she reached him, she leaned in on his other side. "Please, Brandon. Join us." She slid her hand down Brandon's shirt until she reached his hard cock tucked safely in his pants. "Bring him out to play." She kissed his cheek, making him suck in a breath, while at the same time he felt Meredith, his parents' neighbor, stroking his cock as well. He groaned as he felt one of them unbutton his pants while the other pulled his zipper down. Both slipped their hands inside and freed his swollen cock as they pulled him out of the chair and to his feet.

Then he couldn't believe his eyes. Both ladies slid down onto their knees in front of him, their gazes fixed on him. Meredith just grinned up at him as she licked the tip of his cock, the pre-cum gliding over her tongue as she pulled it away. Lindsey lowered her head and started sucking his balls, one hand going to his ass, her fingers digging into his flesh. He groaned just as Meredith swallowed his cock, her tongue twirling around his thick shaft and under the lip of the head. "Oh, god," he moaned as he laid his hand on each of their heads. He couldn't believe what was happening. His neighbor, twice his age, was down on her knees beside his wife giving him the best blow job he had ever had. Two sets of lips kissed and wrapped his cock in their slurps and kisses, making his hard-on pulse with hungry need.

After a few moments of Meredith bobbing her beautiful head on his cock, the ladies switched places, and Lindsey took his cock in her mouth, following the older woman's example. Meredith knee-walked around him, kissing his thigh and then his ass, her hands on his waist as she whispered, "Such a good boy you are, Brandon. Standing still and letting us have our fun. And you taste so good. God, I've wanted to feel your cock in my mouth for so long."

He groaned at her words as he watched Lindsey devouring his cock, one hand gripping the base of his shaft as she bobbed her head back and forth. He thought for sure he would blow his load soon, but she pulled her blond head off him just in time, smiling up at him as she licked her lips. "Meredith is right. You taste great."

"I think it's time, our boy here returned the favor, don't you, Lindsey?" Meredith stood, taking Brandon's shirt in her hands and pulling it over his head as Lindsey pulled his pants the rest of the way down his legs and off his body.

"Oh, definitely," Lindsey said.

Once Brandon was as naked as the two women, Meredith led them all over to her sofa, pulling Lindsey down beside her as she tugged Brandon down to his knees. She then leaned back, legs open, revealing the pinkest slit slick with her juices. Reaching out, she pulled Brandon's head down between her legs until he could smell her pussy, and then, she shoved his face down onto her cunt, ordering him to lick her.

Brandon obeyed, diving into her wetness as he glided his tongue up her slit to her swollen clit, sucking the tight pearl into his mouth and flicking his tongue over it. He gripped her hips, holding her tight as he tongued her, her wetness covering his mouth. Glancing up, he watched as Meredith pulled Lindsey down to her left breast, ordering the younger woman to suck her nipple. Brandon's cock throbbed as he watched his gorgeous wife lean down and take the older woman's nipple in her mouth, sucking it like a newborn. Brandon groaned, wanting desperately to touch his swollen manhood but not wanting to stop pleasuring the woman in front of him. There was no way he would do anything to derail what was happening in his neighbor's house right then. He never imagined that his fantasies would become real or that his wife would be a participant, but there the three of them were, naked as the day they were born, while two of them pleased the older woman with everything they had.

Brandon ran his tongue up the wet slit of Meredith's pussy, sucking her juices into his mouth, thinking he was the luckiest man alive.

Meredith's moans filled the small living room, and he felt her hand on his head, shoving his face harder onto her pussy. He could see Meredith's other hand on the back of Lindsey's head as she whispered to his wife what a good job he was doing. "We should definitely give him some reward, don't you think?" she asked his wife.

Lindsey just moaned, never pulling her mouth from the woman's breast.

Meredith glanced down at him. "Yes, I think so, too. I'm sure his cock is begging for release."

Brandon just groaned.

FIVE

Meredith took a handful of his hair and pulled him from her pussy as she pushed Lindsey onto her back. Slipping from the sofa, the older woman lowered herself to her knees, positioning herself between the young blond's thighs as she turned to face Brandon. "I do hope you're ready to use that cock of yours." She then lowered her head to Lindsey's pussy, who didn't even look at him as she watched the woman going down on her.

Brandon knelt there a moment, watching as Meredith's tongue ran up the length of Lindsey's slick slit, tasting his wife and making her squirm. Lindsey moaned as she stretched her arms out along the couch, pressing her pussy up into Meredith's face, grinding it on the other woman's tongue.

Meredith wiggled her ass at Brandon, enticing him to lay claim to the treasure that waited for him between her legs. This opportunity would not go to waste. He moved over to stand behind his neighbor, kneeling down once he stood between her legs. However, he couldn't rush this moment, not knowing when he would get the chance again. As he kneels there, he can't help but run his hand over Meredith's well-tanned ass, enjoying the curve of her hip, the feel of her flesh as he dragged his fingers along her backside. With a deep breath, he glanced up and Lindsey is watching him, her eyes glazed from the pleasure their neighbor is giving her. He smiles at his wife, grabs Meredith's hips, and slams his cock into the older woman's tight hole. Meredith moans into Lindsey's pussy, and his wife just grins at him, her eyes begging him to fuck the other woman.

He slams into their neighbor, his hips pounding her ass, his cock spearing into her as her pussy swallowed every inch of his thick manhood. He dug his fingers into her ass, driving into her harder, faster, her whimpers muffled by Lindsey's pussy but still filling the living room. Lindsey had a hand on the woman's head, holding her in place, grinding her face in her cunt. Her breathing grew heavy, and Brandon could see her tits rising and falling with the effort as she shoved her pussy out to Meredith's working mouth. Meredith shoved her ass out to Brandon, meeting his driving rhythm beat for beat as he drove into her deeper and deeper his balls slapping against her clit. He could feel her pussy pulling at his cock, milking him as he fucked her. The living room was now filled with their moans and groans, all three of them giving or receiving pleasure.

"Oh god!" Lindsey screamed out, and Brandon watched her drop her other hand to the top of Meredith's head, holding the older woman in place, her hips smashing up into Meredith's face. "That's it. Right there. Oh, god, lick that clit. Please, don't stop. Please!"

Brandon thrust into Meredith's pussy harder, but his gaze was riveted to his wife as she shoved back on the couch while shoving her cunt up into the other woman's face. He felt his cock throbbing, felt it grow harder inside his neighbor's sweet sex, and he didn't think that was even possible.

"Yes!" Lindsey cried out, her mouth open wide and her eyes clamped tightly shut as her ass lifted off the sofa as she shoved Meredith's face harder into her pussy. "Right there!" Her entire body gave a sudden jerk and then she collapsed into the sofa, melting into a puddle of afterglow.

Meredith kissed the top of Lindsey's pussy and then laid her head on the younger woman's thighs, begging Brandon to fuck her harder. "Drive that cock into me. Faster. Fuck me faster!" She drove back onto him as he gripped her hips and yanked her backward. He felt her body tighten around his cock, felt the juices flood out of her to drip between them. Then her orgasm hit, cascading waves of pleasure that rippled through her and sucked on his cock.

The need to explode built within Brandon, a rising crescendo just before his cock gushed into her. He clasped her hips, pulling her hard into one final thrust before his manhood danced and sprayed, coating her inner walls with his hot sticky love. His grunt sounded loud as she shoved back onto him, wiggling on his shaft, draining every last drop of his passion from his cock as she screamed into Lindsey's thighs.

He held onto her for a moment before collapsing backward, falling onto his heels, his still hard cock slipping from her soaked pussy dragging a trail of their juices with him. His chest heaved with his breathing, and when he glanced up, he saw Lindsey smiling at him, her arms still out to her sides, her body limp with pleasure.

Meredith turned and sat on the floor, one arm draped over his wife's knee as the older woman stared at him, her tits rising and falling with her heavy breaths as well. She grinned at him, and then she leaned down and sucked his cock clean, one hand sliding around his waist to grip his ass. He watched her head bob back and forth, still not believing what had just happened but relishing every second.

When she had sucked him clean, she leaned back on the sofa, returning her arm to Lindsey's knee. Smiling, Meredith said, "Yes, definitely a lot more freedom when you're in your own place." Then her smile turned into a mischievous grin. "Of course, you two can always feel free to come visit your neighbor whenever it starts feeling a little too crowded at your parents' place."

He nodded, still not sure he could talk with the way his breathing controlled him. Yet, he knew they would be visiting Meredith as often as possible. Glancing up into his wife's eyes, he knew she felt the same way as him. Their freedom was just next door.

CAUGHT BY HIS NEIGHBOR

Jared was more than ready for his weekend to begin. The sun was high in the sky, perfect for a dip in the pool or a day at the beach. Of course, going to the beach meant getting in the car and actually leaving the house, something he desperately would love to avoid. Besides, his neighbors, the Wakelys, had given him free reign to use their pool whenever he wanted, and if he was lucky enough, he'd get a chance to see Mrs. Wakely in her skimpy bikini. A closeup view would sure beat sneaking glances at her from over the privacy fence that separated their yard. He had been gawking at her ripe melons and curvaceous ass since he was old enough to understand what the hell he was looking at, using her image in his mind whenever he'd jerk himself off at night. The woman had the hottest body, and it didn't matter to him that she was more than twice his age; that fact only added to his rush.

Grabbing a towel, he headed out his front door, crossing the yard to knock on the Wakelys' front door and enter the world of his fantasies, if only in his mind.

No one answered, so Jared slipped around to the side and let himself in through the side gate, regretting that Mrs. Wakely wasn't there, but still planning on taking full advantage of her empty pool. He draped his towel over one of the chaise lounge chairs on the deck and then eased himself down into the cool water. The surface was warm enough, but just as his nuts hit the water, a chill shot up his body, covering his flesh in goosebumps until he managed to get all the way in and soaked. His body didn't take long to become accustomed to the water, and soon, he was doing a few laps in the pool, allowing the water to propel him back and forth with each downward arc of his arms. The sun felt amazing beating down on his back as he glided across the water.

Once he had worn himself out with his laps, he flipped over on his back and just floated along the pool's surface, allowing the sun to warm his chest and face. He thought of Mrs. Wakely as he floated there, how her ass fit inside her tight gym shorts, and her breasts seemed to just flow over the top of any shirt she wore. He would love to get a glimpse of her sex, the slit that he dreamed about as he stroked his cock off when alone in his bed at night. He would love to be the one to sink his rod deep into the valley between her legs, watching those massive tits of hers bounce and jiggle with each thrust. He wondered if she was a screamer when she was being fucked, or just a quiet woman who held her breath, trying not to let on that she enjoyed it. He hoped she was a screamer. He wanted to know she enjoyed it if he ever got the chance to drive into her.

The more he thought of fucking Mrs. Wakely, the harder his cock became, until the bulge in his bathing suit was quite noticeable. With his eyes closed due to the sun, he slid his hand into his trunks, gripping his stiff rod and stroking it, his mind still on his neighbor's luscious body. He felt his cock grow even harder as he masturbated, needing relief after so many lustful thoughts about his hot neighbor. God, he wished he had the guts to just go up to her and kiss her, to stretch out his hands and grab her massive tits, to tweak her perky nip—

"Jared Johnson!" he heard Mrs. Wakely scream. "What the hell do you think you're doing?"

He yanked his hand out of his bathing suit, his legs dropping underneath him, but not quite touching the pool's bottom. He felt himself going under, the water swallowing him as he dropped below the surface. When he finally managed to get his feet under him and stand, he stood there staring at Colleen Wakely, her arms crossed over her chest as she glared at him. She wore a light sundress with a low neckline, her creamy globes busting out of the top. The dress hugged her curvy hips, and he was sure the fabric was snug on her heart-shaped ass. He caught himself following her long legs down to her feet in her tan sandals before he jerked his gaze back up to her face. "Um, high, Mrs. Wakely," he stuttered, lowering his hands in front of him to try to hide his raging hard-on. His embarrassment reddened his face as he stood there in front of his neighbor, not sure what to do at the moment. "I didn't hear you come out."

"Oh, that was quite obvious," she said with a sneer. "Too busy with your hand toying with that dick of yours, it seems, to remember you were in my pool while you played with yourself. Is this a habit of yours? Jacking off in other people's pools?"

"No, Mrs. Wakely," he said, the words coming out in a rush. "I promise. I don't...well...this was the first time...I'm sorry. Please don't tell my parents or Mr. Wakely. Please. I'll do anything." Panic gripped him, wondering what her husband would do to him if she told him how she had caught Jared playing with himself in their pool. Or worse, his father! God, he would be in so much trouble.

"And why shouldn't I tell them?" she asked. "Someone should deal with this type of behavior, don't you think?" She glared at him, daring him, it seemed, to disagree with her.

He needed an alternative, so he just blurted out the first thought that came to his mind. "You could do it. You could punish me. Please, Mrs. Wakely, don't tell anyone. I'll agree to whatever you want to do to me. I swear."

She arched an eyebrow at him. "Anything?"

He nodded vigorously. "Yes, ma'am. Whatever you want, I'll

do." Would she actually punish him? As twisted as it sounded, the thought caused his cock to stir back to life once more.

She continued to stare at him for a moment as if debating whether his idea was a good one or not. Seeming to have made her decision, she told him to get out of the pool and to stand by the lounge chair.

As Jared climbed out of the pool, his hands still in front of his hard cock trying to hide it, Colleen moved over to one of the chairs and took a seat, stretching out her shapely legs. She glanced over at him as she sat down. "Oh, please, move your hands, Jared," she snapped. "I think the time for hiding is now over, don't you?"

He blushed again as he nodded, dropping his hands to his sides. "Yes, ma'am," he said weakly as moved to stand in front of her. "I'm sorry." He was quite aware of how his cock strained against his bathing suit, begging to be taken out and toyed with again.

She stared at his bulge as she sat there, debating within, it seemed, what to do with the young man in front of her. "So, what should I do with you?" she asked, but to herself, not Jared. She glanced back into his eyes, her brows pinched with curiosity. "What had you so horny that you had to touch yourself in my pool?"

Jared shifted where he stood, not wanting to answer her question and get himself in any more trouble. "I, um, was just having a fantasy," he finally told her, hoping she wouldn't press the issue.

"A fantasy, huh?" she tilted her head to the side as she studied him some more. "And just what were you fantasizing about?"

Shit! "Do I really have to answer?" he said, almost whining the question.

"You did say anything, didn't you?" she reminded him. "Consider this part of anything." She held up a finger. "But only a part. There will be more."

"Yes, ma'am," he sighed. He took a deep breath, swallowing the nervousness that filled his throat. "I was fantasizing about you and your body." He wanted to close his eyes and hide. To admit such a thing to his neighbor in this way was more than embarrassing; it was humiliating.

"About me?" she pressed. "And just what about me and my body were you imagining?" Now she looked more curious than pissed, and somehow, that gave Jared a little bit of hope that his punishment wouldn't be as bad as he feared. "And don't lie to me, Jared. That will only make your punishment worse."

He nodded, his arms hanging limply at his sides, his cock throbbing in his bathing suit. How his cock was still rock hard, he had no idea. The humiliation alone should have shriveled his member up and sent it hiding. "I was picturing things I would love to do to your body. It's gorgeous, and I've always wanted to touch it. I pictured worshipping it with my mouth and hands."

She cocked an eyebrow at him again. "And not your cock?"

He took another deep breath. "Yes, ma'am, even with my cock. I pictured making love to you, and it made me so horny I just had to touch myself." He then started rushing his words again. "I'm sorry, Mrs. Wakely. I swear I didn't know you were here. I would never have been so brazen if I had."

She ignored his panic. "And do you jack off to images of me often?"

He nodded, realizing that she was in no way going to make this easy on him. He surrendered to his fate. "Yes, ma'am. All the time since I started to have boners."

"Wow," she said, almost as if impressed. "That long, huh?" She nodded her head slowly. She then smirked at him, her lips twisted in a more seductive manner. "And would you like to touch my body, Jared? Run your hands over my breasts and suck my nipples? Is that what you really want?"

Oh, god, he couldn't believe what she was asking him. "Yes, ma'am," he admitted, figuring he had already admitted so much already, why not go all the way with his confession. "Yes, ma'am. I would love to worship your body."

She nodded once as if thinking over his answer. "Maybe, but do you really deserve it after allowing me to catch you diddling with yourself?"

Jared hung his head, seeing his chance to fulfill his fantasy slipping from his grasp. "I'm sorry, Mrs. Wakely. Truly, I am." He feared to look at the older woman and see the disgust in her eyes.

"I can leave and never bother you again."

"Oh?" she asked. "I thought you agreed to my punishment."

He jerked his head up, staring at the woman, his mouth open. "Yes, ma'am. Whatever you want." He needed to get through this humiliation so that she didn't tell her husband or his parents.

She nodded. "Very well then. Let's get the punishment out of the way, and if you handle it well, we'll see if I allow you anything else." She stared at his hard cock. "First, however, you need to get rid of that bathing suit." She stared at him, one eyebrow cocked as she waited for him to carry out her order.

He wasn't sure what to do, so he just stood there. Could she really want him to strip in front of her? Didn't she just yell at him for masturbating in her pool? Now she wanted him naked?

She sighed. "Jared, this isn't going to go well if you don't listen to me and follow my orders. I've already seen your hand wrapped around that cock of yours. You might as well let me see the whole thing. Now, strip."

Jared didn't need telling twice. He pulled the string on his bathing suit, ripped the Velcro open, and slid his trunks down his legs, his raging boner popping out long and straight. After kicking his suit to the side, he stood in front of his neighbor, completely exposed and praying Mr. Wakely didn't come home early.

With raised eyebrows, Colleen raked her gaze over his young body, fixing her eyes on his hard shaft as he stood there, arms back at his sides. He saw no sense in hiding his cock again. She had demanded to see his manhood, and he would obey her now no matter what she asked of him. Of course, what she demanded next shocked him.

"Are you ready for your punishment?" she asked as she reached down and removed one of her sandals.

He stared at her with wide eyes as he nodded, not trusting his voice to speak.

"Good," she said as she shifted in her lounge chair, sitting up straighter, pressing her legs together as she pulled her sundress up to uncover her legs. "I think an old fashioned spanking is in order."

"A spanking?" he asked, not sure he liked the idea of being paddled by his neighbor. No one had spanked him since he was five years old for crying out loud!

"A spanking," Colleen repeated. "You will lay across my lap, ass up in the air, and I'm going to spank you with my sandal until I think you've learned your lesson. It's either that or I tell your parents what I caught you doing. Which will it be?" She just stared at him waiting for an answer.

Jared didn't see where he had a choice. Suffering the humiliation of being spanked by this gorgeous woman was preferable to what his parents would think of him or what her husband would do to him if he ever discovered Jared's sin.

With a slow nod, he walked to the side of the chair, lowered himself to his knees, and draped himself over the older woman's lap, embarrassment reddening his cheeks—both sets more than likely. He could feel his hard cock rub against her bare legs, and almost groaned at the touch, his mind torn between the shame of what was about to happen to him and the lust he felt with his cock on her skin.

"Now, you are not to enjoy this, so don't think I'm going to take it easy on you," she told him. "You will not move or cover your ass with your hands until I am finished and tell you that you can get up. Is that understood?"

"Yes, ma'am," he said, his voice shaking.

"Good boy," she purred, and then he felt her hand caressing his bare ass, her touch light as she stroked his flesh. "God, but you have a gorgeous ass. So firm and tight." She squeezed one of his ass cheeks. "It's going to be fun seeing how red it gets." And then, before Jared knew what was happening, he felt the bottom of her sandal smacking his rear, making him yelp with surprise as well as pain. His body jerked slightly, and he felt his cock rub against her legs. He groaned from the friction. "I said you were not to enjoy this, Jared," she repeated as she smacked his ass again, the sandal hitting both of his ass cheeks.

Colleen then smacked his ass several times, and every time her sandal hit him, his body rocked across her lap, his cock rubbing back and forth as if he was masturbating. He couldn't help but groan again as she spanked him, his ass already on fire as she beat him, his body rocking back and forth across her legs. If his neighbor knew what was happening, she didn't show any signs of it. She kept spanking him, forcing his body to wiggle in her lap, making him move as if he humped her leg.

"Mrs. Wakely," he started to warn her, but she shushed him. He tried all he could to stop his cock from exploding, but with how horny he had been in the pool and with the rocking back and forth across her lap, he couldn't keep his cum from spewing out of his shaft and across her thighs.

"What the hell?" she screamed smacking his ass one more time, harder than any of the others. She then shoved him off her lap. "I told you this was not to be enjoyment, you pervert. How dare you! Look what you did!"

He stood beside her chair, his face crimson with his embarrassment. "I'm sorry, Mrs. Wakely," he stammered. "I tried to say something, but you told me to be quiet. I'm sorry. Really sorry." His ass burned from where she had spanked him, but he was afraid to rub it.

She shook her head as she glanced down at his cum covering her legs. Reaching over, she snatched his towel off the chair beside her and cleaned herself up. "Well, it shouldn't surprise me," she said with a sigh. "You are still a young man, unable to control your passions very well from what I witnessed when I walked in on you a few moments ago." She glanced up at him, her gaze falling to his cock that was finally starting to shrink. "Well, you got yours." She looked back up into his eyes. "Now, it's my turn to get mine, don't you think?"

He looked at her, confusion bunching his forehead. "I'm sorry? I don't understand."

Colleen swung her legs off the side of the chair and stood to her feet, grabbing the hem of her sundress as she did. Jared could only stand there and watch as she pulled the dress up her sleek body and over her head, dropping it to the ground when she was through. He just stared, soaking in her beautiful flesh, her round perfect breasts with their dark aureoles and swollen nipples, her flat stomach, and the deep valley between her legs that glistened with her wetness. Suddenly, Jared understood, even though he still hesitated to believe his luck.

She sauntered over to where Jared stood, his arms still dangling down at his sides. Running her fingers across his chest, and then down to the happy trail that led to his still semi-hard cock. She gripped his cock, stroking it as she leaned in and kissed his neck. "Are you ready to give your neighbor her orgasm and fulfill your fantasy?" She kissed him again as she led him back to her chair by his cock.

Jared sucked in a breath as he followed her to the chair and watched her sit back down, her hand still gripping his manhood. She pulled him down to his knees beside her, snaked a hand behind his head and pulled his mouth to her breast. "Here you go, neighbor," she purred.

Jared parted his lips and devoured her tit, sucking her nipple into his mouth, flicking her swollen bud back and forth with his tongue. He slid an arm over her waist, running his hand up her side and then over to her other mound, massaging the large melon as he sucked her nipple, her hand toying with his hair.

"Oh, god, yes," she cooed in his ear, her breathing growing more ragged as he twirled his tongue around her nipple. "That's perfect. Keep making me feel so good. Was this your fantasy? Is that what you saw when you stroked that cock of yours?"

He nodded, murmuring his ascent, but not taking his mouth from her tit. He wasn't going to stop until she made him stop, afraid he'd never get another chance to have her breast in his mouth again. This was the culmination of years of fantasies, and his cock was already rock hard again.

She squeezed his head, pushing him downward. "Don't forget my pussy, Jared," she purred. "I'm sure you've fantasized about tasting my sweet sex. I want to feel your tongue."

Jared groaned at her words as he started to kiss his way down her slender body to the sweet valley between her legs. He breathed in her sultry aroma, relishing how close he was to her pussy. Sliding between her legs so he had a better angle, he kissed the top of her mound, licking around her hard pearl before gliding his tongue down between her folds tasting her honey. He couldn't help but moan at the joy of eating her cunt as he slid his hands up her sides, toying with her breasts as he ravished her pussy with his mouth.

Colleen wiggled under him, shoving her cunt up into his face as she slid a hand into his dark hair, gripping it in her fist and grinding her sex against his lips. "That's it, Jared," she cooed from above him. "Tongue that pussy like a good boy." She draped her legs over his shoulders, wrapping her thighs around his head as she squeezed him to her. "God, your tongue feels so good. Shove it into my pussy. Taste it. That's it."

She kept grinding on his face as Jared hungrily lapped at her pussy, her juices coating his lips and chin. He shoved his tongue into her entrance, fucking her with it before sliding it back up to her swollen clit and sucking on her bud like a woman would a cock. He gripped her hips tighter as he ate her pussy, her body squirming underneath him as she clamped her thighs on his head tighter.

"Right there, Jared," she cried out. "Don't stop! Don't you dare fucking stop!" Jared felt her body tense in his grip as she shoved her cunt up into his face, pressing his mouth to her tighter. Then Colleen started to shake, her hips twisting as her orgasm washed through her making her body rock as she arched her back.

Jared kept sucking, running his tongue back and forth over her clit as she came into his mouth, her wetness gushing over his face. She clamped her thighs against his face so hard, he thought she'd snap his neck as she thrashed about on the chair, but he never let go or stopped licking her clit.

After what seemed forever, she collapsed back onto the chair, her body relaxed, her breathing coming out in ragged gasps as she grinned down at him. "You are definitely earning my forgiveness," she said with a husky voice. She bounced her eyebrows at him as she bit her lower lip, basking in her orgasm.

Jared grinned up at her, pleased that he had gotten her off with his mouth. Her juices coated his face, and his cock throbbed between his legs as he decided being punished had never been so much fun.

Colleen crooked her finger at him, motioning for him to come stand beside her again, a grin plastered on her face.

Jared slid off the lounge chair, his cock sticking straight out and throbbing with his need. Within seconds, he stood beside her, arms at his sides as he waited for her next instructions.

Colleen reached out, taking his thick rod in her hand and stroking it back and forth. "Such a good neighbor to take care of me this way," she said as she leaned forward and licked the pre-cum that pooled at the tip of his dick.

Jared moaned as he watched her, relishing the visual as well as the feel of her tongue on his manhood.

She glanced up at him, winked, and then swallowed his cock, her lips devouring his shaft until he could feel the back of her throat. He watched her head bob back and forth on his cock, mesmerized that she was even doing it. "God," he moaned, not sure what to do with his hands, still nervous that this could all end suddenly.

He shouldn't have worried, however.

When Colleen took her mouth from his cock, a small strand of saliva stretching between them, she grinned up at him. "Are you ready for the rest of your fantasy?" she asked.

His eyes widened as he watched her shift on the chair, getting on her hands and knees. Her giant tits swayed under her, luscious in their movements. "Oh god, yes," he whispered.

She glanced over at him, gesturing to her rear with a nod of her head. "Fuck me, neighbor," she ordered. "Pound that thick cock of yours into my married cunt."

"Yes ma'am," he said, excitement filling his voice as he walked around behind her. He straddled the chair as he gripped her waist, the head of his cock at her entrance. With one hand he gripped his shaft and eased the tip to her opening while she watched him over her shoulder.

"Fuck me, Jared," she urged. "Now!"

He thrust into her, burying his cock balls deep inside his neighbor's married pussy. Colleen cried out, dropping her head to the chair as she pushed her ass back against him. "Oh, god, you're so fucking big," she moaned. "You feel so good. Fuck me harder, Jared. Faster!"

Jared continued to pound into her, driving his meaty rod in and out of her soaking cunt. He knew with everything that had happened, he probably wouldn't last long. Her pussy sucked on his cock, her cunt walls gripping him tightly as he fucked her, sucking him deeper into her. He thrust harder as she begged, his piston splitting her wide before him.

She gripped the sides of the chair with white knuckles as she bounced back on his cock, meeting each one of his thrusts. The backyard filled with her mewling sounds as he fucked her, the chair squeaking underneath them. He felt his cock twitch and knew he was about to empty his load into her married pussy. He willed himself to hold out, but just before he shot his spunk into her, she screamed, shoving herself back onto his meaty shaft once more as she cried out, "I'm coming! Oh, god, Jared, I'm coming on that young cock of yours!"

He couldn't hold out any longer and felt his cock explode into her drenched pussy as her body shook in his grasp. His cum filled her cunt, their juices pouring out of her to drip down her thighs and onto his balls. She whimpered as she wiggled on his cock, her whole body one tight cord in his hands.

When her orgasm finally subsided, she fell forward, laying flat on the chair in front of him while he stood there, his cock dripping their juices. He could see her gaping slit, the wetness of both of them at her entrance, and he couldn't keep the grin from his face. He had fucked his neighbor—bucket list checked.

He shifted so he no longer straddled the chair, standing for a moment to catch his breath before sliding into the chair beside her, watching her.

Colleen opened her eyes and stared at him with a glazed expression. She gave him a satisfied grin. "I'm so glad you grew up," she said.

He chuckled slightly. "I'm glad you caught me playing with myself," he told her. "Best punishment ever."

She giggled. "I'll have to invite you over and punish you some more."

He smiled over at her. "Whatever you want," he assured her. "I mean, what are neighbors for, right?"

THE COUGAR NEXT DOOR

Tommy stepped out into his backyard, ready to finish fixing the back fence his mother had been harping on him to repair since he returned from college three days ago. Not exactly what he wanted to be doing with his little mini-vacation, but with his father gone thanks to a big-busted secretary, Tommy was the one left holding the hammer. Luckily, the day wasn't overbearingly hot, and his neighbor gave him permission to use her pool at any time. That was something he would definitely be taking advantage of even though the pool wasn't exactly what he wanted to be dipping into while he was home for a brief visit.

With the hammer gripped firmly in hand, he stepped up to the fence to fill in the missing planks. He paused, however, when thoughts of his neighbor entered his mind and glanced over the fence to her backyard. Mrs. Clemens had lived next door to them ever since he could remember, her husband having passed away several years back. Tommy had spent his puberty years jerking off to fantasies of his neighbor and her large breasts that always seemed to be straining the fabric of any shirt she wore, her nipples poking out like tiny pebbles. She also loved to wear those tight yoga pants whenever she worked out in her yard, and Tommy had found his gaze constantly drawn to her heart-shaped ass on more than one occasion. If she ever noticed his gawking, she never let on, always offering him a smile whenever he caught her eye. She was a gorgeous woman, of that there was no doubt, which confused him as to why he never saw her with another man. Surely, she had needs just like anyone else.

Turning back to the task at hand, Tommy gripped his hammer and started pounding nails into the fence planks, the entire time wishing he was driving his own hammer between Mrs. Clemens' darkly tanned thighs.

As the day wore on, the sun grew higher and hotter, sweat beading up on Tommy's brow, making his shaggy hair stick to his scalp. He had shed his shirt halfway through the job, now standing out there in just his shorts, the sun baking his skin. By the time he finished repairing the fence, he was more than ready to take advantage of Mrs. Clemens' pool.

After putting his tools away, Tommy grabbed a towel and went to knock on his neighbor's front door. When no one answered, he walked around to the side gate and let himself into her backyard. The sun sparkled on the pool's surface, and he wasted no time tossing his towel onto one of the chaise lounge chairs along the pool deck and diving into the deep end. The water was cold, at first, but his over-heated body quickly grew accustomed to it as he swam around, allowing the water to lower his body temperature and cool him off. After doing a couple of laps in the pool, he flipped over onto his back and floated for a while, the sun warming his face while the water kept him relaxed and cool.

Tommy wasn't sure how long he floated there, but when he opened his eyes again, the sun had crossed half the sky. Figuring he needed to get out and return home to check on his mother, he dipped his legs under him and stood in the shallow end of the pool. After wiping the water out of his eyes, he froze a minute, noticing Mrs. Clemens sitting on the edge of the pool watching him, her feet dangling in the water as she smiled over at him. He couldn't help but stare at her for a moment, her tanned flesh barely covered in her two-piece bathing suit, her nipples straining against the fabric as her massive tits oozed out the sides. Even though she was sitting, he could still see the dark flesh of her ass peeking out the bottoms of her bathing suit from the side.

Suddenly, he worried that he had overstepped. "Um, hey," he said, weakly. "Sorry, I didn't hear you come out. I hope you don't mind. You had said I could use your pool whenever I wanted."

She smiled over at him, waving off his apology. "I did, and I meant it," she said. "I'm glad you took advantage. It's a beautiful day for a swim." She gestured to her bathing suit. "I saw you out here and thought I'd join you. I hope you don't mind."

He raked his gaze over her body again before catching himself and jerking his eyes up to hers. "Not at all," he said quickly, hoping she hadn't caught his gawking. "Always nice to swim with someone else."

She nodded as she slid off the side of the pool and down into the water. "I agree," she said just before she dunked under the surface, soaking her entire body and getting the shock of the chill water out of the way.

Tommy just watched as her dark blond hair disappeared only to pop back up a second later a little closer to where he stood. He was glad he was under the water and visibility wasn't that great under the surface as he could feel his cock starting to stiffen just by watching his neighbor. He ducked a little lower in the water, hoping the bend in his legs would help hide his growing rod even more. He didn't need this gorgeous woman thinking him some kind of young pervert.

When Mrs. Clemens broke the surface again, her long hair stuck to her scalp and fell down her slender back, Tommy almost groaned. Her bathing suit appeared almost see-through. He could swear he saw her naked breasts under the fabric, the dark circles of her aureoles shriveling into tiny discs around her stiff nipples, which were even more prominent in her drenched bathing suit. He couldn't take his eyes off of her as she ran her hand over her hair, straightening it out and getting the stray strands out of her crystal blue eyes. He had to remember to close his mouth, he was gawking so much.

She smiled at him when she opened her eyes again, allowing herself to float closer to him. "And how are you enjoying your stay?" she asked. "Glad to have a break from classes?"

Tommy swallowed the dryness of his throat as he nodded. "Um, yeah, anytime away from school is good," he said, finally able to speak without sounding like some high school kid. "How are things around here?"

She shrugged, her arms sliding back and forth in the water as she allowed herself to drift closer to him. He couldn't help but notice the way the water lapped at the tops of her tits, splashing lightly between her thick cleavage. "Every day around here is just like any other," she said. "Not a lot going on. How about with you back at school? Driving the girls mad with those arms of yours? Looks like you've been working out. I bet you keep the girls pinned close, don't you?"

He chuckled a little as he watched her drift even closer. "To be honest, I haven't had much time for dating. Classes have been pretty tough this semester."

"Now, Tommy, you know what they say," she cooed in his ear as she swam beside him, turning to face him, her body close enough that he could feel her warm breath on his face. "All work and no play makes Tommy a sad boy. You need to get out there and unwind, relax, cut up, and definitely get laid." She slid her hands up his arms to his shoulder when she said that last part.

Tommy started coughing with her last phrase, choking on his reaction. He had never known Mrs. Clemens to be so blunt. Or so touchy-feely.

The older woman slid a hand down from his shoulder, gliding it over his firm chest toward his abdomen. Tommy stood frozen, unsure what to do. Hoping her hand would stop while praying that it wouldn't.

His prayers were answered.

Mrs. Clemens' hand glided over his stomach and down his happy trail to the bulge he could no longer hide in his bathing suit. She gripped his hard shaft, stroking it up and down with gentle movements as she stared into his eyes. "Um, Mrs. Clemens..."

"Please, Tommy," she said, her voice a husky whisper. "I think you can call me Jamie now, don't you? Mrs. Clemens seems so formal while my hand is stroking this magnificent cock of yours. God, I never realized how big you would be. And you're not giving this to any lucky girl on campus? That's sad. They don't know what they're missing."

He could feel his breathing growing heavier the more she stroked. He still wasn't sure what to say or even do, so he just stood there, allowing the other woman to jack him off through his bathing suit. The fact that his neighbor, the one he had masturbated to growing up was actually right then fulfilling some of his fantasies almost made him blow his load just by her touch. This was almost too much to be real.

With a deep breath, he decided to go for broke. After all, if she was stroking his dick, there wasn't much that could go wrong at this point, right? He slid his hands around her waist, allowing them to glide down her back until he cupped her ass, the ass he had dreamt of all throughout high school. He closed his eyes, relishing the feel of her firm ass cheeks in his hands. He massaged her sweet rear, and she rewarded him with a moan of her own.

"Now, I was hoping I wouldn't scare you away," she said. Then she grinned up at him. "You know, this would be a lot more fun without the bathing suits. I usually don't wear them anyway when I'm out here."

Tommy watched as she released his cock, reached behind her, and pulled the string on her bikini. He couldn't take his eyes off her breasts, his cock throbbing in his suit as he anticipated the big reveal. She kept staring at him, but his gaze remained fixed on her hardened nipples as she slid the bathing suit top down and off.

He almost shot his load right then, her massive mounds out for his pleasure, her dark aureoles puckered tight around her hardened pebbles. He didn't wait for her to tell him what to do next. He reached out and caressed one tit while he lowered his mouth down to the other, sucking her nipple into his mouth and flicking it with his tongue. He felt her hands in his hair as she moaned in his ear. "God, yes," she purred. He sucked a little harder, his other hand massaging her giant globe, barely able to fit her entire tit into the palm of his hand. Her breasts were even more gorgeous than he had imagined.

He felt her hands slide back down to his crotch, heard the Velcro on his suit being ripped open, and then felt her hand on his throbbing cock. She stroked his aching rod down to its base, and then cupped his balls, massaging them as he massaged her breast. He sucked in another breath around her nipple, his tongue twirling over the tight bud in small, slow circles.

"Oh, god, Tommy," she whimpered in his ear. "I need to feel you. Your cock is so fucking big. I want it." She pulled his head back from her breast, her eyes glassy with lust. "But first, I want your mouth." She kept her grip on his cock, his bathing suit sliding down his legs, as she walked him to the edge of the pool. Once they reached the side, he kicked his bathing suit the rest of the way off, allowing it to float off on its own. She turned to him, and with a devilish grin on her face, reached down to her bathing suit bottoms and slid them off her voluptuous legs.

He just stared, her bald pussy glistening under the water's surface. She turned again, lifted herself up onto the side of the pool, and spread her legs in front of him. Leaning back, holding herself up with the palms of her hands, she just grinned at him. "Come and get it," she said.

Tommy just stared at her slick slit, her pussy folds begging for his mouth. He moved to where she sat, his hands sliding up her thighs as she spread her legs wider for him. Wetness dripped from her cunt, and not just from the pool. Tommy yearned to taste her nectar. With a deep breath, he inhaled her musky scent, never imagining that he would ever be between her legs like he was. Then, he lowered his mouth to her pussy, gliding his tongue up the side of her fold and then back down the other, teasing her cunt. Once he reached the bottom of her sweet pussy again, he divided her folds with his tongue and licked his way up again until he found her tight pearl. He sucked her swollen clit into his mouth, shoving the hood back with his tongue and flicking her sensitive button back and forth.

Jamie moaned as she shoved her cunt onto his mouth, one hand sliding to the back of his head and holding him in place as she ground her cunt on his face. Tommy kept licking, sucking her clit, and feeling her squirm under his machinations. He gripped her thighs tighter, holding her in place as he ravished her entrance with his mouth, tongue-fucking her and savoring every drop of her sweet honey. She gripped his head tighter, humping his face now with her pussy, her thighs tight around his head as her body started to shudder.

"God, Tommy, right there," she moaned. "Whatever you're doing, don't stop. Eat that cunt. Lick it. Oh god!"

His cock throbbed with every word she uttered. He licked her faster, his tongue flicking back and forth over her clit and lapping down her folds. This was more than he had imagined, and he was not going to disappoint the woman.

Her body shook with her first orgasm, and he could feel her fist his hair, the pain sharp, but he wasn't about to stop no matter what. She cried out, her legs clamped around the sides of his face as she almost smothered him with her cunt.

Then, all at once, she released him and settled back, her giant tits rising and falling with her heavy breaths as she released his hair. She smiled down at him as she licked her lips. "Now, that was amazing," she said. "I love that tongue of yours."

He grinned at her. "Glad you liked it," he said, sheepishly. "I definitely enjoyed being down there."

She giggled. "Good., but now it's your turn." She slid down off the side of the pool and into the water, taking Tommy's hand in hers. He allowed her to lead him over to the steps where she made him sit on the top one, his raging hard-on just poking out of the surface of the water. He watched as she lowered herself to her knees on the bottom step, taking his thick rod in her hand. Glancing up at him, she said, "Would it surprise you to know that I have thought about this moment a lot since you left for college?" She glided her hand up and down his hard shaft, her grin growing bigger. "I've masturbated to your image between my legs."

Her words shocked him, but not as much as watching her lower her mouth down onto his cock, licking the tip, twirling her tongue around the head, and then swallowing his huge manhood into her mouth. He groaned, almost loud enough for the other neighbors to hear, and then caught himself. He couldn't take his gaze off her bobbing head as she twirled her tongue around his lengthy shaft, gliding over the rigid veins as she sucked him off. Harder, she sucked him, her head moving quickly, the air filling with her slurping noises. Tommy gripped the sides of the pool, the warm water lapping around his thighs as Jamie sucked his cock, one hand going to his balls and toying with them between her fingers. God, this was better than his fantasies!

He could feel his cock throbbing in her mouth and panicked that he would come before he could sink his cock into her wet cunt. His groan must have warned her, because Jamie pulled her mouth from his shaft, a long string of saliva stretching from the tip of his dick to her lips as she pulled away, grinning. "God, I love the way your cock stretches my mouth," she said. "I can't wait to feel it stretch my pussy. Do you want it, Tommy? Do you want my pussy?"

"Oh god, yes," he said, almost groaning the words.

She just grinned at him as she moved from between his legs and started to climb the steps in front of him until she straddled him. "Good, because I want to feel that monster cock of yours inside my horny cunt." With one hand gripping his shoulder, she reached between them and took his throbbing cock in her hand, guiding it to her hungry channel as she lowered herself down into his lap.

Tommy held her waist, watching her pussy swallow his cock, her breasts gliding across his face as she sunk down onto him. He took his eyes off their crotches and started sucking her nipple, doing his best to devour her breast with his mouth, while he slid his other hand down to her ass, gripping it tightly.

Her pussy engulfed his cock, making her gasp as she speared herself down onto his giant manhood. She then started to rock back and forth, her clit rubbing against his pelvic bone as she gripped his shoulders with both hands again. He could only hold on as she rode him, her giant tits in his face, his tongue flicking her swollen nipple. This is what he had jacked off to for so many years and now it was happening. God, he'd be jacking off so much more now, he knew, with these images in his head.

He was so close to coming, he gripped her ass and held on tight as she continued to rock against him, but just as he thought he was going to explode, Jamie stopped, gripping his hair and yanking his head away from her nipple.

Her face filled with passion, her eyes glazed, as she stared at him. "I want you to take me from behind," she said, already sliding off his cock. She leaned against the side of the pool, her amazing ass shoved back to allow Tommy to drive into her from behind.

He didn't waste any time. He scampered off the steps and moved behind her, his hands gripping her waist as he felt her ass sliding up and down on his cock. Gripping his meaty shaft, he teased her entrance just a bit, parting her folds before shoving his cock back into her cunt.

Jamie cried out, her hands clutching the side of the pool as she shoved herself back against him. "That's it," she groaned. "Fuck that cunt, Tommy. Pound me."

He squeezed her hips, digging his fingernails into her flesh as he rammed her again and again from behind, his thick shaft spreading her pussy open before him as he thrust into her. She cried out, urging him to go faster, to fuck her harder. "Don't be gentle, damn it! Fuck me!"

He could see her tits sliding against the side of the pool, the redness from the friction spreading as he continued to drive into her. She cried out over and over, begging for more of his manhood. He shoved it into her, her juices coating his cock, the pool water splashing up around them as he fucked her. He was going to come soon, he knew, but he kept thrusting into her, not wanting to finish before her.

Then her body shuddered, her ass shoving back against him, wiggling on his thick shaft. She made one long wail as her whole body seemed to suck his cock, her pussy walls gripping his shaft tight as she came. She pounded the pool wall, shoved herself back onto him harder as he gripped her hips.

And then he couldn't hold back any longer. His cum erupted from his cock, filling his neighbor's pussy with his younger passion. She moaned again as he emptied himself in her, glancing over her shoulder, a sinister grin on her face. "God, yes" she groaned. "I wanted that, I wanted your young cum." She wiggled her pussy on his cock again, giggling. "God, it feels so good."

He grinned back, her words stirring him even more as he felt his cock slip from her pussy. He almost apologized, but she stopped him, turning and gripping his deflating manhood in her hands. "Don't worry about it," she said as she nuzzled into his neck. "We've got plenty of time to make him come out and play again."

Tommy groaned as she felt his cock stirring once more with her strokes. "That was awesome," he moaned as he glanced down into her eyes, his breathing still ragged gasps. "I have wanted to do that for years."

Jamie grinned up at him. "So have I," she admitted. "And now that I've had it, I plan on having it more and more."

Tommy just grinned at her. He was definitely going to have to come back on vacation more often.

THE NEIGHBOR'S BACK DOOR

"You volunteered me?" Brandon couldn't believe his ears. His mother knew he had plans that weekend with his buddies out at the lake. He had been looking forward to it ever since Jason told him he had convinced those girls from the sorority to join them. The entire weekend was bound to be one giant sex-fest, and now his mother was telling him he would have to miss it.

"There will be other weekends," his mother said as she stood by the dining room table folding clothes. She stopped and faced him. "I know what you college boys planned on doing this weekend, and I'm sure there will be plenty of opportunities for you to sow those wild oats of yours another time. Joan doesn't ask for much, and she needs the help since her husband left. It's just a few repairs. If you get them done quick, I'm sure you'll be able to join your friends later."

"Right," he groaned. "When everyone is already paired up, and I'm stuck with the leftovers. Great."

"Brandon Randall, that's the rudest thing I've ever heard," his mother snapped. "You do not treat women that way."

He forced himself not to roll his eyes as he murmured a "Yes, ma'am," and sulked into his bedroom. There went his weekend. He could feel his dick shriveling up in disappointment.

Helping his neighbor wasn't the issue. He actually enjoyed visiting Mrs. Carter. She was a little older than his mother, but he didn't think of that whenever he saw the woman. Joan Carter was one of the hottest women he knew with an ass he would love to sink his cock into as he gripped her from behind. Her breasts were globes of perfection, and he loved when she wore her low-cut tops that left the upper portions exposed. She never wore padded bras, so her nipples were pert and protruding for his delight. Several times growing up, he had jacked off to images of holding a fistful of her long blond hair while he drove into her doggy style, sometimes even taking that sweet back door of hers as she moaned in front of him. He never lasted long with that image in his head and usually shot his load quickly.

Of course, he knew there was never a chance of his fantasies coming true, and now he had to suffer with daydreams while his friends were getting real pussy wrapped around their peckers. Life was so not fair.

He switched out of his jeans and shirt, choosing to dress down for his handyman work. Perhaps his mother was right, and if he finished the repairs Mrs. Carter needed, then he could hurry out to the lake and salvage something of his weekend. He would definitely try his damnedest to make it happen.

After slipping on some sweats and an old T-shirt, he said goodbye to his mother and went next door.

Mrs. Carter opened her front door, and suddenly Brandon felt his cock stiffen inside of his sweats. She wore tight yoga pants that hugged her hips and ass in ways he had dreamed of since he met the woman. She also wore a low-cut tank, which hugged her body, without a bra, her nipples already hard and straining against the fabric. She wore her long, blond hair pulled back in a tight ponytail, and her lips looked ready to swallow a cock and bring it to life. His neighbor oozed sexiness, and Brandon suddenly forgot about the lake and his friends. Forcing himself to look into her eyes and not gawk at her tits, Brandon said, "Hello, Mrs. Carter. Mom said you needed some work done around the house."

Joan opened the door wider to let him in, her hand holding the door in a way that her hip jutted out in a sultry manner. "Thank you, Brandon. I appreciate you coming over and lending a hand. I hope I didn't steal you away from anything important."

Deciding to keep his pouting to himself, he answered, "Nothing important. I'm happy to help out." He smiled as he stepped past her and into the house, hoping she hadn't caught the disappointment in his voice. At least he would have the pleasure of staring at her in her tight clothes to distract him from the college girls he could be snuggling up against right then.

"Well, I appreciate it," she said as she closed the door and led him further into her home. "I promise, it's nothing major, some lose trim really, and my back door is having trouble opening. I told your mother not to worry about it. I'm sure I could have found a handyman to come out and do it."

He followed her into the kitchen, his gaze glued to her ass as it swayed in front of him. "No need for that when you have neighbors next door who can help."

She picked up a piece of paper from the counter before turning to him again. "You're a sweet young man, Brandon," she said as she handed him the paper. "I do appreciate this. These are the minor repairs I need. Tools are in the garage, and if you need anything that's not there, just let me know, and I'll get it."

"Yes, ma'am," he said, taking the list and scanning it over. Nothing seemed too difficult, and he figured he could have it all knocked out before too much of the day got away from him. "I'll get right on these."

She thanked him again and then left him to the repairs.

There weren't many: Some trim needed replacing, the back door knob was loose, the door sticking against the frame, and the gutters needed cleaning out. Simple things, really, but Brandon was glad to help her out although he would have loved seeing her up on the ladder, her ass at eye level. He shifted his growing cock in his sweats and counted down from ten, hoping his boner would disappear before Mrs. Carter saw it. He needed to save the fantasies for when he wasn't so close to the object of those fantasies.

As he finished replacing some trim around the hallway doorframe, he heard Mrs. Carter walking up behind him. "Care for some lemonade?" she asked.

He turned, noticing the tall, thin glass of lemonade in her hand where she held it even with her breasts. He couldn't help but stare at her hard nipples pressing against her shirt. Swallowing the lump in his throat, he forced himself to glance up into her eyes. "Thanks," he said as he reached for the glass. As soon as he took it, he downed half of the lemonade, not because he was thirsty, but to give himself time to calm his racing heart. Pressing his lips together when he finished, he nodded once and thanked her again. He then gestured to the trim. "That was the end of it," he said. "I finished the repairs, and cleaned out the gutters. Your back door even opens easier now. You're all set."

"That's great," she said, smiling and crossing her arms over her chest, covering her breasts much to his disappointment. "Do you have time for me to fix you a sandwich or something, or do you have plans for the rest of the day?"

Brandon glanced at his watch. Two o'clock. He still had plenty of time to get a shower, change clothes, and get out to the lake to bang one of the college girls. However, glancing at Mrs.

Carter, he suddenly didn't feel like making the trip. He gave her another smile. "A sandwich sounds great. Thanks."

He followed the older woman back into the kitchen, moving to the sink to wash up as she pulled the sandwich fixings out of the fridge. He glanced over his shoulder at her just as she bent over to pull something out of the bottom drawer, her yoga pants stretched tight against her ass, making it quite apparent she wore no undies underneath. He bit back the groan that threatened to slip past his lips as he jerked his attention back to the sink and washing his hands. If only he could get her out of those pants.

Once he finished washing his hands, he slid into a chair around the kitchen table and watched as she fixed each of them a sandwich.

She smiled over at him, her full lips sending a swelling to his cock he had to shift in the chair to hide. "So, tell me the truth," she said. "What did I really keep you from doing today by having you help me with these repairs?"

He shrugged, trying to make it seem like no big deal. "I was just going to join my buddies out at the lake," he told her. "We had some girls coming over. I'd probably be getting drunk right now and making poor life choices with some girl I barely knew."

She dropped her hands to the counter as she stared at him, her eyebrows down-turned to match her frowning lips. "So, basically, I kept you from getting laid," she said as if she truly felt sorry for him not being able to sink his cock into some girl he had just met.

"I'm sorry. You should have said something. I remember those days when you could be wild and carefree without worry."

He wasn't sure how to take her comment, or her sympathy, so he just waved it off. "It's no big deal. Really," he assured her. "I was more than happy to come over and help. There will always be other weekends and other easy girls."

She chuckled as she pointed the butter knife at him. "That's your mother talking," she said. With a shake of her head, she returned to the task at hand. "She probably wanted you to be here to keep you from doing something she didn't approve of." She glanced back over at him as she placed the lunchmeat on the bread. "Trust me, I know how prudish a mom can be with their children."

"It's not like I'm still in high school," he said, sounding more annoyed than he wanted. "I'm over halfway through college, and Mom knows I've had sex before, so the fact that's what I was heading out there for shouldn't shock her."

Joan put the sandwiches on plates and carried them over to the table, setting them down before sliding into a chair across from Brandon. Her breasts were right in his line of sight, the soft swells of her melons pushing out the top of her tank top. "You're still her baby boy in her eyes," she told him. Then her grin grew as she added, "Even if the rest of us see the hot man you've become."

Brandon shifted slightly in his chair, his cock twitching at the way his neighbor looked at him. He wasn't sure what to say, so he just lifted his sandwich and took a bite.

The rest of the meal went by with idle chitchat. How are things going at college? Was Brandon serious about anyone? Was anyone serious about him? The litany of inquisitiveness continued until they had devoured the club sandwiches and two more glasses of lemonade swallowed. He laughed, and Mrs. Carter...well, if he wasn't crazy, Mrs. Carter flirted with him. Several times throughout the meal, Joan—she insisted that he call her by her first name—reached across the table and touched his arm as she laughed at something he said, smiled a little longer than normal, and stared at his lips with a lingering gaze that drew him closer and kept him in his seat.

Once they finished eating, Joan took the plates and empty glasses to the sink, Brandon's eyes glued to her ass as she sashayed across the floor. "You know, I feel bad," Joan said as she scraped the plates and put them in the sink.

Brandon felt his brows pinch in confusion. "About?"

The older woman turned, her lips pushed into a slight pout as she crossed the room to where he sat. "I caused you to miss all the action going on out at the lake," she told him. When she reached him, she turned him slightly so he faced away from the table and slid between his legs, her hands going to his shoulders. "Right now, you could be all naked with one of those college girls sucking that bulge in your sweats I've noticed today, and instead, you're here with me doing repairs. It's not fair."

Brandon swallowed the lump in his throat, unsure of what to

say or where to even put his hands with Mrs. Carter so close. If she noticed his hard-on before, she was definitely getting an eyeful now as there was no way he could keep his cock flaccid with the hot woman between his legs, touching him. "It's all right," he assured her, his voice weak as he tried to stare up into her eyes and not at her swollen nipples pressing against her tank top. "I don't mind. Really. I was happy to do it." He sounded like an idiot, he knew, but her close proximity made him nervous and horny as hell.

"Now, now, you don't have to lie, Brandon," she said as she smiled at him, massaging his shoulders. "You'd probably be around a bunch of naked college girls right now if you weren't here, wouldn't you?"

He licked his lips as he nodded once. "Probably," he said, his voice soft, not sure where his neighbor was heading with her conversation.

"And I caused you to miss it," she said, her voice a sweet pout. "Here. Let me make it up to you."

He felt her hands leave his shoulders, and then she grabbed the hem of her tank top and pulled it over her head and tossed it on the table, her orange-sized breasts staring him in the face, her nipples tight buds of hardness he wanted to suck. He just stared, not sure what to do.

"There," she said. "Is that what you would see if you were at the lake?"

He nodded. "Yes, ma'am. I'm sure they wouldn't be so nice

looking though." He openly gawked at her breasts now. How could he not? They were right there in his face.

"Oh, you're so sweet," she cooed. "But I bet that's not all you'd see, is it?" She cocked her head at him as if she dared him to deny it.

With a stuttering breath, he said, "No, ma'am. I'm sure they'd be naked."

"Well then," she said, and then she had her fingers in the waistband of her yoga pants, sliding them down her firm legs and off.

Brandon couldn't believe what he was witnessing. Within seconds, his neighbor was stark naked in front of him, her hands back on his shoulders as she stared at him.

"I know it's not the body of a college girl, but I hope it makes up for you having to miss your day," Joan said.

"Oh, god," Brandon practically moaned. "Your body is gorgeous." He sat there, hands on his knees, unsure what to do. While his neighbor had just stripped in front of him, it didn't mean she wanted anything else. Did it?

Joan grinned at him. "I bet you'd be sucking their tits, wouldn't you?" she asked as she swayed in front of him, her breasts swinging slightly, teasing.

"Um, I probably would, yes," he said.

"Brandon, I want to make it up to you for missing your day at the lake," she told him. "Whatever you think you'd be doing with those college girls, I want you to feel free to do with me now. Please."

Brandon groaned as she moaned the word please, his eyes focused on her shrunken aureoles and her hardened nipples. He glanced up into her eyes once, still unsure if what she had said was what he had heard. She just moaned another, "Please," as she slid her hand around his neck and up into his hair, pulling his face to her breast.

He didn't need anymore urging. He parted his lips, sucking her swollen nipple into his mouth as he flicked his tongue back and forth over the tight bud. Her moans filled his ears as her grip on the back of his head tightened. As he sucked on her breast, he slid his hands around her waist to cup her tight ass, massaging her cheeks as he worshiped her breast.

"Oh god, yes, Brandon," she groaned as she pressed her ass back into his hands. "That's it. Take me. Whatever you want."

He continued to twirl his tongue over her nipple, stopping only long enough to kiss his way from one breast to the other, running his tongue up and down her cleavage, relishing the taste of her flesh. She pulled at his hair, moving his head around in tight circles as she forced his mouth against her breast harder, demanding he suck her harder. He flicked his tongue over her bud, his fingers dipping into her ass crack and toying with the entrance of her dark hole. She groaned even louder.

Brandon could feel his cock throb inside his sweatpants,

straining against the fabric as Joan rubbed her thigh back and forth on it as he continued to suck her tit. He moaned around her nipple, his tongue twirling in slow circles. He worried she would cause him to explode before he saw how far his neighbor would allow him to go and tried to adjust his cock where he sat, but her touch felt so good, he didn't want it to stop.

However, Joan pulled his head away from her breasts as she slid back a little. Her grin grew more seductive as she glanced down at him. "You know, I bet those girls would do more than just let you suck their titties," she said as she slid down to her knees between his legs.

Brandon just stared at her, not believing what she was doing. Was his neighbor really going to do what it looked like? He sucked in a breath as she reached for the front of his sweatpants, reached in and pulled out his raging hard-on. He groaned as she wrapped her hand around his cock, still staring at him as she did, biting her lower lip.

When she glanced down at his manhood, she licked her lips. "Now, that's a thick cock," she purred.

Brandon watched as she lowered her head, running her tongue over the tip of his shaft and lapping up the pre-cum that had pooled there, twirling her tongue around his velvet helmet. He felt himself shift in the chair, sliding more to the edge to give her more room. He gripped the side of his chair, not sure what else to do with his hands as she ran her tongue down his length, sucking at his base just before gliding her tongue back up to his tip. She glanced up at him once, winked, and then swallowed his cock until he felt the head hit the back of her throat. With one hand she gripped the base of his hardness, while with the other, she toyed with his balls, massaging them between her fingers.

Brandon did his best to sit still, his arms tight cords of muscle as he held onto the chair, but he found it difficult with his neighbor sucking his cock. He could only sit there and watch as her blond head bobbed up and down on his shaft, his cock throbbing in her mouth as she ran her tongue over every ridge and vein. He felt his hips thrusting up to meet her mouth even with his attempt at sitting still. It was almost as if she sucked his ass up off the chair as she deep throated him. His cock throbbed, and he feared he would shoot his load in her mouth, but just like last time, she seemed to know just when to stop, keeping him from coming.

With one last lick up the underside of his cock, she glanced up at him, her lips swollen from the blow job she just gave him. "I bet you'd return the favor for them, wouldn't you, Brandon" she asked as she stood, moving over to the kitchen table. He watched as she slid up onto the hard surface, her ass at the edge as she spread her legs open for him.

He stared over at her wet slit, her pussy lips glistening as she leaned back on her elbows. He licked his lips as he slid around to face her pussy. With his hands wrapped under her thighs and holding her legs, he leaned in and kissed her wetness before running his tongue up between her wet folds.

Joan moaned as she slid a hand to the top of his head, gripping his hair with her fist and shoving his face down into her cunt. "That's a good boy, Brandon," she purred as she ground her pussy against his mouth. "Make your neighbor feel good. Show her how sweetly you'd treat those college girls."

Brandon glanced up to see Joan lying all the way back on the table, her hand still gripping the top of his head tightly. He closed his eyes and inhaled her musky scent as he licked up one fold and down the other, tasting her sweet honey. He shoved his tongue into her drenched entrance, tongue-fucking her for a bit before running his tongue up to her swollen pearl, sucking the tight bud into his mouth.

She cried out as she thrust her hip against his mouth. "That's it, Brandon," she moaned. "Right there. Keep that up. Oh god."

He sucked on her clit, flicking the tight bud back and forth with his tongue as he slid a hand from her thigh to her opening. Her wetness poured out as he shoved two fingers deep into her cunt, curving them slightly to touch that sweet spot at the top of her pussy. He pounded her cunt with his fingers as he continued to suck her clit, her body bucking against his face as her thighs tightened around his head. She pulled his hair tighter, almost making him yelp in pain, but he continued to ravish her pussy with his mouth and fingers.

"Another!" she cried out. 'Give me another finger."

He obeyed, adding a third finger as he fucked her pussy, his knuckles hitting her wet folds. He sucked her clit, tonguing her pearl and sending her body into jolts of shivers. Then he felt her clamp her legs against his head, squeezing as her body tightened into one taut knot.

"There! Oh god, there! Right there!" she cried out, and her body shook with her orgasm. She gripped his head and shoved her cunt up into his face, almost smothering him as she ground against his mouth. "I'm coming! Damn! Coming!" The last was more a grunt than a cry, and Brandon held onto her trembling legs as Joan's orgasm flooded her, causing her to rock back and forth, her legs pressed against the side of his face. By the time her orgasm subsided, her sweet nectar covered Brandon's face along with a satisfied grin.

Joan leaned back up on her elbows as she grinned down at him. "That was intense, but I bet you wouldn't have stopped there with those college girls, would you?"

Brandon had no doubt that things were about to get even sweeter. "No, ma'am," he admitted. "I'm sure after that, I'd be sinking my cock into their soaked cunts."

She grinned at him as she slid to the edge of the table a little more. "I hoped you'd say that," she admitted, spreading her legs wider and just looking at him. "So, fuck me, Brandon. I want to feel that young cock of yours buried deep in my pussy."

He didn't need her to tell him twice. Standing, he slid his

sweat pants down his legs and off and then stepped between Joan's legs, gripping her thighs and lifting them slightly in the air. She watched him, biting her bottom lip as she reached down between them and took his massive cock in her hand, guiding his manhood to her slick channel. He glanced down, the sight of his shaft disappearing between her folds almost causing him to shoot his load right then. With one deep thrust, he buried his cock into her pussy until his balls slapped her ass cheeks.

Joan groaned, reaching back and placing her palms on the table as Brandon continued to hold her legs up into the air and against his chest. He pounded into her, driving his shaft back and forth into her wetness, the sounds filling the kitchen. He couldn't take his eyes off the way her tits bounced as he thrust into her and reached out with one hand to tweak one of her swollen nipples. She moaned, glancing down at him as he drilled into her. "God, yes," she said. "Again. Harder. Please."

He pinched her nipple, twisting the swollen nub slightly in his fingers as his hips pounded her thighs as he fucked her. She groaned louder as she pounded her palms on the tabletop, rolling her head side to side. His cock throbbed, and he slowed a little, fearing he would come too soon.

Joan grinned at him, leaning up and placing a hand on his stomach. "I want you in my ass," she said, waggling her eyebrows at him. "Have you ever fucked a girl there before? Did those college girls let you take their dark star?"

He felt his eyebrows pop up as he shook his head. "No," he admitted, sliding his cock out of her wetness. Fucking a girl's ass was always something he had wanted to do, but no one had ever given him the chance yet. That his neighbor was begging for it right then made his cock throb even more.

As soon as he stepped back, Joan rolled over, sliding so that she stood, bent over the table's edge. She grinned back at him over her shoulder. "I love coming this way," she told him. "Do you want it? Do you want my back door?"

"Oh god, yes," he moaned as he stepped back up to her ass, spreading her sweet cheeks and positioning his cock right at her dark hole. Her wetness had dripped down her ass crack, coating her with her juices, and his cock was already slick from her pussy. He took his cock in his hand, guiding it to her tight star and pressing it in gently. With a deep breath, he thrust into her, her ass fighting him a bit, until he felt it pop past her tight ring and bury itself into her ass.

Joan cried out, gripping at the table as she shoved herself back against him. "Oh god, yes!" she cried out. "That's it, Brandon. Take my ass."

Her back door was tight as he pounded into her, slipping his cock out and shoving it back inside of her. She thrashed on the table as he drove into her, fucking her, his hips beating her ass, her moans and groans filling the house. "Keep fucking me, Brandon. Harder. Fuck my ass hard."

He watched as she slid a hand down between her legs, rubbing her clit as he fucked her, his hands gripping her waist as he pulled her back and forth onto his shaft.

"Faster," she demanded. "Fuck that ass!"

His cock throbbed inside her as he shoved his piston in and out of her tight hole, her ass sucking at his cock as she rubbed herself off.

"God, your cock is so big," she panted. "Almost there, Brandon. Keep fucking me with that gorgeous young cock of yours."

He could feel her ass tightening around his cock as he pounded her, his fingers digging into her hips. Every once in a while, he could feel her fingers hit his balls as she rubbed herself off, making his cock throb even more. This was definitely better than going out to the lake.

"There!" Joan shouted. "Oh god, I'm coming!" She grunted as she shoved herself back on him.

He gripped her hips and held her tight against him, her ass sucking his manhood until he felt his own orgasm explode from his cock, filling her dark hole with his passion. He grunted, her back door milking his shaft of his seed, as she cried out, both of their bodies one tight knot of sexual tension that had just emptied itself, their breathing heavy in the small kitchen.

Once his legs stopped trembling, Brandon eased back, giving Joan room to move. A quick glance at her ass, showed her star winking at him, his cum dripping from the dark hole. Her pussy lips glistened, wetness dripping down her thigh.

Joan shifted, turning herself so that she could ease down into one of the kitchen chairs, her breasts rising and falling with her own heavy breathing. With one arm, she leaned on the table as she smiled over at him. "Now, I hope that made up for you missing your time at the lake."

He grinned, nodding, as he sat down in the chair closest to her. "More than made up for it," he assured her. "I'd much rather do this than hang out with a bunch of college girls."

She reached out and took his hand in hers, squeezing it. "Well then, we're just going to have to make sure you get your chance." She squeezed his hand one more time and then stood. "I need some water. How about you?" She turned and walked to the fridge.

"That would be great, thanks," he said, his gaze fixed on her bare ass as she crossed the kitchen. He needed to make sure he thanked his mother for forcing him to help their neighbor. Best repair job ever.

Joan pulled two water bottles out of the fridge and walked back over to the table. "Thanks for fixing my trim," she said with a wink as she handed him the bottle. "You really know how to use that hammer of yours."

He took a long swallow, his eyes on her breasts as she sat back down. Setting the bottle back on the table, he smiled over at her. "Trust me, it was my pleasure. I'm free all day, so whatever else you need…" He let the rest of the sentence hang in the air, hoping she would catch his meaning.

She grinned at him over the rim of her bottle. "Oh, I'm sure we can find more things for you to pound."

Brandon just grinned. It always paid to be neighborly.

AN EYE FOR TEACHER

ONE

Tricia knew parent-teacher nights were important, but really? For kindergarten? How bad could her daughter be to fail milk and cookies? Tricia shifted in her seat next to her husband, Drew. He didn't seem as annoyed as she to be there, not seeing it for the waste of time it truly was. Not her Drew. Oh no, he *wanted* to be there. He saw it as his parental duty to be as active as possible in his daughter's life, even though it was just kindergarten. Kindergarten! Tricia sighed. *What? Did little Lacy not stay within the lines while coloring?* And to make matters worse, the teacher—a Mr. Landon Turner—was late. How could he demand a meeting and then be late for it? Of all the inconsiderate, rude, obnoxious… He wasn't a doctor, waiting on several patients at once. If this was some sort of power play, Mr. Landon Turner would soon learn she didn't play games well. Besides, Tricia didn't understand why the man was a kindergarten teacher to begin with. He was thirty-five from what she had heard, not some doddering old man or young whip fresh out of college. So why wasn't he teaching middle school or even high school? What was wrong with this man?

"Sorry for being late," a deep voice sounded from behind them. "I had to show the last set of parents to their older son's classroom." A tall man with short, dark hair and biceps that stretched the sleeves of his dress shirt, walked around the desk they sat in front of, dropping some papers on the top as he smiled down at them with the darkest chocolate eyes Tricia had ever seen. His smile brightened the room, whisking her sour mood out the door as he reached an arm out to shake Drew's hand, and then her own. "Your little Lacy is a laugh a minute," he said as he settled into his seat. "I've really enjoyed having her in my class. She's well-behaved, always uses her manners, and always wants to help the other kids. You've made my job easy this year."

"Our Lacy?" Drew said, feigning shock. He then chuckled. "She always tries helping her little brother do things around the house. She's a good little girl."

Tricia didn't say anything, but rather just stared at Landon, Mr. Turner. His hands were thick, powerful, and she could imagine them covering her entire back as he pressed her against his massive chest, pinning her to the… Tricia shook her head. She did not need to be fantasizing about her daughter's kindergarten teacher, especially at parent-teacher night. She cocked her head, suddenly confused. "I'm sorry," she said, "but you don't strike me as a kindergarten teacher. I was kind of expecting a more... Well, an older man, at least."

Landon didn't seem offended at all by her statement. He just nodded his head as he laughed. "I actually get that quite a lot. However, my favorite teacher when I was a kid was my kindergarten teacher, a very southern, elderly lady with the thickest accent." He chuckled, shaking his head. "I still don't think I can count to five without a heavy drawl on the word five."

Tricia really wanted to hear him say the number five, so much so that she felt the wetness pooling between her legs.

He shrugged, still smiling. "So, I decided to teach kindergarten and try to emulate my teacher. I see it as the foundation that might help them enjoy the rest of their school career. If I can give them the best experience possible, then they might not grow up hating school and learning."

"Well, Lacy is eager every morning to come to school, so you have to be doing a great job," Drew said. "Hopefully, you're still teaching when our son starts school."

Tricia echoed that sentiment. She was definitely ready for another parent-teacher night with Mr. Landon Turner. Of course, she also pictured being held after class with him, serving detention, just the two of them. *Oh god, would he paddle me?*

"Right, Trish?" Drew asked, but for the life of her, she

couldn't remember the question. She just smiled and nodded, hoping whatever she agreed to wasn't too bad.

"Well, it was great meeting both of you," Landon said as he stood, arm extended toward Drew, hand out. "I look forward to teaching your daughter, and please, if you ever have any questions, feel free to drop me an email." He gripped Drew's hand, shaking it, and then reached over to shake hers.

She panicked, at first, worried that her hands would be sweaty or clammy, but she reached across the desk and took his hand anyway, this time feeling the strength in his grip as he squeezed her hand. She took a deep breath, imagining those fingers delving deep within her sex, pumping in and out of her, bringing her to the brink... She took another deep breath. "And if I can do anything to help you, please just let me know. Anything at all." She smiled, hoping he would take her up on her offer.

He smiled back. "I will, thank you." That glint in his eye made her heart beat faster.

Drew led her out of the classroom, through the school, and toward the car. "Well, I think that went well," he said once they were outside the school. "I like him."

Tricia bit her lower lip before saying, "I like him, too."

TWO

Tricia envied her daughter when little Lacy left for school. She wanted to be the student in Mr. Turner's class, sitting in the front row, staring at the bulge in his pants as he sat on the corner of the desk, legs slightly parted. She took a deep breath, trying to calm the sudden twinge that made her pussy ache. She could only imagine the reactions of the girls if Landon taught high school. He was definitely safer teaching kindergarten, and Tricia was the lucky one. She needed to figure out how to volunteer more for his class, maybe offer to be class mom or something. Oh, how she would love to be his volunteer.

Little Bradley was still asleep, Drew was off to work, and Lacy was at school, leaving Tricia some free time to take her fantasies into her own hands. Or her own fingers as the case may be. She fell asleep last night with visions of Landon Turner filling her mind and making her pussy drip; the thoughts making her grind her clit against the bedsheets as she laid beside her husband, him none the wiser as he snored away. She had wanted to slip her fingers between her legs while she laid there, but somehow that seemed a little too risky, so she had tried to sleep, tried to put Landon's strong hands and thick shoulders out of her mind. Tried, but to no avail. She spent a long, frustrating night tossing and turning, scolding herself for her fantasy and what her daughter's teacher had done to her with just one parent-teacher meeting. Now, with a quiet house, she needed to relieve some of her pent-up frustration, and she intended to make the most of her time.

She locked the doors, poured herself another cup of coffee, and headed for her bedroom and the small vibrator that hid in her nightstand drawer. She needed it, the throbbing ache between her legs told her that, urging her to the bedroom until she splayed herself out on the bed. After grabbing her toy, she stacked some pillows up, ready to brace her for her time of satisfaction. She then stripped, for this was not going to be a quickie with her panties twisted at her knees. No, she wanted this, wanted to savor every pulsing twitch of her vibrator.

Once she was naked, she spread herself out on the bedspread, her legs slightly parted as she leaned back on the pile of pillows. She closed her eyes as she ran one hand down her neck, gliding her fingers over her breast until her hardened nipple ached to be touched. She took the sensitive bud in her fingers, twirling it back and forth, twisting and pinching as her back arched, shoving her breasts up into the air. However, they weren't her fingers she saw twisting her nipple, but rather, Landon's long, thick fingers. She imagined she could feel his warm breath on her breast as he toyed with her, fanning the embers of desire within her into roaring flames. A moan slipped from her lips, and she pinched her nipple harder, sending tendrils of pleasure-pain throughout her body. She could feel the wetness grow between her legs, the sweet pleasure valley growing hungrier and hungrier, begging to be filled, toyed with.

Spreading her legs a little wider, she slid her other hand down her stomach to the pearl at the top of her pussy, rubbed her clit in small circles as her breathing started growing heavier. She bit her lip as she rubbed harder, faster, feeling her hips moving up and down with desire. With her eyes closed, she saw Landon's dark hair as he lowered his head to her pussy, his tongue gliding out across her flesh, tasting her for the very first time. She whimpered, her breathing faster, her moans louder as she slipped a finger into her soaking slit, pumping it in and out as she used her thumb on her clit. Twisting her fingers around her nipple again, she heard herself begging for him to take her, to use her for his own pleasure. Being a teacher, she wondered if he had any fantasies that involved punishing a naughty girl in a school uniform. *God, I need to get a plaid skirt.*

Desire burned through her until she couldn't take it anymore.

She reached to her side, grabbing the vibrator. With a quick flick of the switch, she heard the vibration kick into high gear, the buzzing sound filling the bedroom, and her breathing caught in her throat. Her chest rose and fell with her panting, her nipples catching her gaze. She felt the flush flooding her body as she placed the toy on her clit and pressed down, her mouth popping open as a moan ripped from her lips.

She saw Landon sliding his body up hers, felt his cock tease at her entrance just before he shoved it deep inside of her. "Yes!" Her back arched, her hand left her nipple and gripped the bedspread as she continued to feel the pulsing of her vibe pleasure her, saw her fantasy driving into her, fucking her. God, she hoped this was his idea of detention for her. She would stay after school every day, begging for his discipline.

And his cock.

Her body tightened, her breathing grew deeper as a shuddering began to wrack her body, her orgasm washing through her. She screamed and didn't even realize until her orgasm had subsided that she had called out Landon's name.

THREE

Drew came in through the front door just like always, briefcase in hand. "Did you see the moving truck across the street?" he asked, dropping his briefcase on the kitchen counter. "Looks like we finally have a new neighbor."

Tricia had to admit she hadn't seen the truck. She did hear one earlier, but forgot about it as soon as the sound vanished. Their three-year-old usually kept her hopping around the house, forcing her to use his nap time to get as much cleaning done as possible while she had the chance and quietness. "Did you get a look at who it is?" she asked. "Hopefully, it's not some crotchety old man who bitches at kids if they get on his grass."

Drew chuckled as he leaned in and kissed his wife lightly on the lips. "You're safe on the old man part. Actually, you won't believe who it is. You should go take a look. He's unloading his car now."

"I don't want to look like some snoopy neighbor, Drew." She couldn't believe he had suggested such a thing. "I'm sure I'll see him in due time. He is right across the street after all."

"Okay, if that's how you want to play it, but don't say I didn't try to get you to go look."

"Mommy! Daddy! Did you see my teacher across the street?" Lacy ran into the kitchen, her little legs and arms pumping with her excitement as she crossed the room.

Tricia cocked her head to the side as she stared at her daughter. "Your teacher?" She then glanced up at Drew, her eyes narrowed slits of disbelief. "Landon Turner is our new neighbor?"

Drew just stood there grinning like the Cheshire Cat as he nodded his head. "Yup."

"Why the hell didn't you tell me?" She wiped her hands on a towel before tossing it to the counter. She checked her hair in a mirror that hung on the wall near the doorway before rushing out of the kitchen toward the front door.

"Why didn't I..?" Drew stood in the middle of the kitchen as she left the room. "I tried to tell you," he called after her. "You didn't want to be bothered, remember?"

She didn't respond as she entered the living room, heading for the front door, passing Bradley, who was lost in his Hot Wheels cars, on her way. Just before she opened the front door, she paused, took a deep breath, and licked her lips to moisten them. *Slow down, girl, and don't look like an idiot.* With another deep breath, she opened the door, turning her lips up into a smile as she stepped out into the afternoon heat. Sure enough, there was Mr. Landon Turner, dressed in shorts that revealed his powerful thighs and a T-shirt that hugged his chest in the same way Tricia wanted to hug him, pulling a box out of the trunk of his car, his biceps bulging with the weight of the box. Tricia felt the heat pool between her legs at the sight as her mind fantasized about how those arms would feel holding her.

Landon glanced up, noticing Tricia as she walked down her long driveway toward the street. He smiled as he closed his trunk and set the box on top, draping his arm over the top as he watched her walk toward him. "Well, hello there," he said as she crossed the street and started up his drive. "I'd say what a small world, except that seems so cliché."

She giggled as she slid her hands into her back pockets, nodding as she glanced down at her feet. "Yeah, I couldn't believe it when Lacy came into the kitchen screaming that you were across the street. I guess now you won't have to go far to ask me to volunteer for something in your class." She glanced back up at him as she spoke, still smiling.

He laughed, the deep sound making her stomach flutter as her body quivered. God, she was acting like a high school girl with a crush, but she couldn't help it. Landon Turner was a man to drool over. "No, I guess I don't," he said, still chuckling. Then he looked up and down the street. "So, how's the neighborhood? It seems rather quiet. Peaceful."

"Oh, it is," she said. She then spent the next few minutes giving him a rundown of the neighbors and some of the city's events. Their town was a quaint place, which was why her and Drew chose to move there when they started having a family. The streets were safe for kids to ride their bikes on or play a game of street ball. Cops regularly patrolled the neighborhood, keeping the mischief and crime down. Most of the neighbors looked out for each other, even having a block party around the holidays. "It's a perfect town to raise a family in if you and your wife have kids." *God, was that too obvious? I hope I wasn't being too obvious.*

If she was, however, Landon didn't let on. Instead, he just smiled as he gave a shake of his head. "No kids and no wife. At least, not yet. Hell, I'm not even dating anyone, so hopefully, being a confirmed bachelor isn't a negative around here."

Tricia giggled at his words as she shook her head. "Not at all. We welcome everyone with open arms." *And god, how I would love to open my legs for him.* She knew she shouldn't be having these thoughts. After all, she was a married woman, but something about Mr. Landon Turner had her juices flowing and her pheromones kicked into high drive. Even masturbating with images of him pounding her this afternoon hadn't quelled the wetness that had soaked into her panties at the sight of him. If anything, it only added to her torment. Drew would be getting fucked hard tonight, just so she could release some of her pent-up frustration. It didn't matter that her husband wasn't the one who got her in that state; he'd be the one to help get her out of it.

She realized she was staring and neither of them had said anything for a couple of minutes. Feeling embarrassed, she quickly stammered, "Well, I'll let you finish unpacking. If you need anything, you know where we are." She pointed to her house across the street as if he hadn't just watched her walk over a few moments ago. "Feel free to knock anytime."

He nodded once. "I will. Thanks."

She backed up, waving, the butterflies in her stomach working overtime, before turning and walking back to her own home. God, she was going to go nuts looking at his body every day.

FOUR

Once the kids were asleep, Drew poured them both a glass of wine, and they settled down on the sofa, soft jazz playing in the background. She could tell by the smirk on his face that he had something on his mind and was just waiting to tell her what it was. She took the offered glass of wine, taking a sip before she leaned back on the sofa, waiting for his comment. She knew it wouldn't be long. If Drew had something on his mind, it always came out, even if it shouldn't.

"So," he started, his smile visible around the rim of his glass as he took a sip of the merlot. "You seemed pretty happy to see our daughter's teacher earlier. Should I be jealous?" There was a mischievous twinkle in his eyes, and Tricia could only roll hers. She was not going to play into his warped fantasies even if she was having them herself.

"No, you shouldn't be jealous," she said, disbelief at his suggestion dripping from each word. "I just wanted to make him feel welcomed into the neighborhood, that's all. We know what it's like to be the new family in town."

"Really? Well, that was very considerate of you. I thought, perhaps, you wanted to see what he looked like in that T-shirt that seemed a little too small for him." Drew smirked again as he turned so that he faced her. "You know it's never bothered me if you look at other men. Hell, I look at other woman. Window shopping is fine as long as you don't go to make a purchase."

She laughed as she shook her head. "You're incorrigible, you know that?"

"So I've been told plenty of times. Now, are you going to bake him a cake? Cookies? Offer to have him over after school?" She could tell by his tone that Drew was just teasing her, but each thought made her pussy quiver even more, and she felt as ashamed by that fact as she was excited by it. She had never cheated on Drew, and never intended on crossing that line, but she just could not get the image of those long fingers of Landon's or his powerful arms out of her mind. Since seeing him the other night, she constantly fantasized about being pinned by him as he drove his cock into her.

"Earth to Trish, come in Trish."

Tricia shook her head, shaking the images out of her head. "What? I'm sorry. I must have zoned out. What were you saying?"

Drew just laughed. "Uh huh, not distracted at all by him." He laughed some more as he lifted his glass to his lips.

Tricia shrugged. "All right. I'm distracted by him. Still, I wouldn't cheat on you, and you know it." She gave him a smirk. "Of course, that doesn't mean I won't be picturing him the next time my battery-operated-boyfriend is bringing me to the brink again."

"Oh, I have no doubt," Drew said, setting the wine glass on the coffee table. He leaned into Tricia, nuzzling her neck as he glided his fingers up her belly and to her breast. "You are such a tart in your mind." He kissed her neck, leaving a trail of wet lip prints down her throat and to her chest line. "And in mine as well." He nibbled her neck, his hand massaging her breasts through her shirt. "I love what you do to me."

Tricia felt her breathing turned into jagged gasps as she leaned back into the sofa, giving Drew plenty of access for what he was doing. "I love what you do to me, too." She could feel the heat stir between her legs as Drew continued his way down her chest, his hand pulling up her shirt so he could get at her swollen nipple. He ducked a finger inside of her bra and slipped her tit out, his mouth instantly going to her tightened bud. She felt her breathing getting heavier, felt the wetness between her legs drip as she closed her eyes, Drew's hand becoming Landon's, his lips becoming those of her daughter's teacher. She moaned as she pushed her breast into Landon's—Drew's—mouth, running a hand up his back and into his hair. "God, yes."

Drew twirled his tongue around her nipple, sucking it into his mouth as he gripped her hip, holding her tightly against him. She didn't even feel guilty that she was picturing another man while her husband pleased her. It was just pretend, right? How could that be wrong? Her moans grew louder as she gripped the back of his head tighter.

Drew pulled from her grasp as he dropped to the floor between her legs, his hands reaching for the buttons on her pants. He grinned at her, and she was shocked that the fact that she found their new neighbor cute—okay, sexy as hell—turned him on. She lifted her ass as he slid her pants over her hips and across her ass, pulling them down her legs and off. She watched as he spread her legs, her glistening slit open before his hungry gaze. He glanced up at her, grinning, as he lowered his mouth to her slick heat, his tongue gliding on each side of her folds before slipping down her wetness and back up to her tight pearl. Tricia moaned as she gripped the couch, digging her fingers into the cushion as she shoved her hips up, grinding her pussy onto his mouth.

Drew looked up, her wetness on his lips. "See? I knew that man made you hot." And then he dove back between her creamy thighs, his tongue pressing flat over her clit as he sucked her nectar into his mouth.

With a fist in her mouth, Tricia clamped down, trying her best not to scream and wake the kids. She could feel his stubbled chin on the bottom of her pussy, feel his fingers digging into her ass as he lapped at her cunt. She closed her eyes again, and once more, it was Landon down there tonguing her sex, tasting her sweetness as he fucked her with his tongue. She humped her husband's face, but saw another's, and none of that even bothered her. It was just a fantasy, right?

The wave of her orgasm crashed over her, and she reached down, gripping Drew's head and shoving his face deeper into her pussy as she cried out, surrendering to the sensations that rocked her body. She shuddered, her head rolling side-to-side as her back arched. She bit her lower lip to keep from crying out the teacher's name in her passion.

And then, she collapsed onto the couch, her breathing ragged pants as she opened her eyes and saw her husband kneeling there, pleased with himself. *Just a fantasy, right?*

FIVE

Tricia did her best not to keep peeking out the front windows over the next few days, but found it hard not to try to catch a glimpse of Landon. If Drew noticed her odd behavior, he didn't comment on it. She wasn't sure why she was so aroused by the man across the street, but she just couldn't stop thinking about him, the way he moved, his broad chest and powerful arms, his smile. She had masturbated every day to visions of him taking her. It was driving her crazy.

It wasn't that she hadn't had fantasies before; she had, of course, but never with someone she actually knew. They were always more like representations of ideas or celebrities, even blank faces who said all the right words in her ear while they took her like a little slut. Now, she wanted to be Landon's little slut, and she wasn't even sure it was just a fantasy anymore.

"Come, shoot some hoops with the kids and me," Drew said as he twirled a basketball in his hands. He wore an old T-shirt and a ratty pair of gym shorts she never allowed him to leave the house in.

"Please, Mommy," Lacy said as she stood beside her father. Bradley just pointed to the front door and started walking.

"All right," Tricia said. "Let me change into something I don't mind sweating in, and I'll be right out."

"Yay!" Lacy squealed as she bolted for the front door, almost knocking her brother down in her rush.

"Yay!" Drew mimicked as he winked at Tricia and followed his daughter.

Tricia just laughed as she shook her head and then made her way to her bedroom and a quick change of clothes. She slipped on a tight sports bra that allowed the tops of her breasts to show with a loose tank top over it as well as a tight, silky pair of shorts, the cups of her ass just peeking out of the bottom. She grinned as she looked at herself in the mirror. *Oh, Mr. Turner, let's hope you're home today.* Giving her reflection a wink, she turned to join her family out in the driveway.

The first thing she noticed when she stepped outside was that Landon was across the street washing his car. He wore a bathing suit, and that was all, his ripped chest making her pause a moment and stare. She raked her gaze down his body, not missing one inch of his powerful frame, her pussy stirring as she soaked in his fit physique. She would love to have his hands sudsing her body and spraying her down with his hot…

"You ready to play, babe?" Drew's voice cut into her fantasy.

She turned to him, smiling as she nodded. "I am. Do I get a partner?"

"I'll play with you, Mommy," Lacy said as she raced over to her mother. Bradley just rolled around in the grass.

Tricia glanced once more at Landon. This time, he was glancing back and waved.

She waved back, smiling as she dipped her head, suddenly feeling foolish.

"Here we go," Drew said as he started dribbling the ball, moving slowly as their daughter tried to steal the ball from him.

Throughout the game, Tricia's sole purpose was to attract Landon's attention. She knew it was wrong, but she wanted him to notice her, to appreciate the assets she had to ffer. She bent over without bending her knees, her ass aimed at his driveway as her shorts pulled up her ass cheeks, revealing more flesh than she would standing up. She hoped it even revealed a little bit of her pussy, giving him a fair glimpse of everything. If she had to bend over facing his driveway, she made sure to move slowly, so that her top dangled open, revealing how her breasts ached to be touched by his hands. She felt her honey drip with each gesture she made, even jumping when she didn't really need to so that her tits would bounce with her. She could feel her panties being soaked and wondered if any of her wetness had slipped out to glisten down her legs. Drew would think it sweat, but she knew better. Tricia was hot for teacher and there was nothing she could do to shake the feelings building within her. She was acting like a little slut, and she knew it, a married, little slut. Her pussy dripped even more at the thought of the show she was putting on for another man.

"Seems like you have a good game going," Landon said, jerking her attention to the edge of their driveway.

"These women are brutal," Drew said, laughing. "I think Lacy's a natural."

Landon laughed, the sound deep, bringing a vibration to Tricia's soaked cunt. "I can see that. You need a partner, Drew?"

"Sure," Drew said, tossing Landon the ball. "Just be careful of Trish. She likes to foul a lot."

Landon turned and smiled at her, his eyes twinkling. "I'm sure I can handle her."

Tricia swallowed the words she wanted to say and bit her bottom lip. Then she grinned at him. "Let's see what you got." She waggled her eyebrows at him as she bent down to guard him, her top falling open, giving him a perfect view of her breasts. She suddenly regretted wearing a bra.

Once the play started again, she tried to take the ball away from him, twirling in front of him, keeping her breasts in his face. If Drew wondered about her actions, he chose not to say anything. Lacy ran all over the driveway, and Landon even made sure to let her "steal" the ball from him once in a while. As the game progressed, Tricia found it harder to keep her eyes off Landon's bare chest and the way his muscles rippled as he moved, how tight they became when he shot the ball or passed it, the way his cock moved in his bathing suit. At one point, Tricia stumbled and almost fell. Landon was closest and reached out, grabbing her and keeping her from landing hard on her ass on the driveway. It took her a moment to regain her balance, and she pressed herself against him as she did, his cock hard and thick in his bathing suit. She glanced up into his eyes, and he just stared back at her.

She grinned as she bounced off of him, making sure he knew she felt his cock, and stood to her feet again. "Thanks," she said. "That would have hurt."

He dipped his head in a nod. "My pleasure." And then, his voice so low, she knew only she could hear it, he added, "As you can tell, I'm sure." He then turned, and Drew tossed him the ball. It was Landon's turn to shoot.

SIX

Before the basketball game ended, Tricia made sure to invite Landon over for a cookout as a welcome-to-the-neighborhood gesture. "You don't need to bring anything but yourself," she had said. "We'll provide everything. Is there any type of beer or alcohol you prefer?"

Landon had shrugged. "Nah, I'm pretty agreeable with just about anything. What time would you like me here?"

"Seven sound good?" she asked, and she couldn't keep her nervousness down from the thought that he would be in their home tonight, casual, drinking. She knew Drew would never go for it, but she could fantasize. She fantasized a lot.

"I'll be here," he said and walked off to shower and get ready. Tricia envied the water that would be touching his firm body.

As it neared seven, Tricia suddenly remembered they were

out of butter and sent Drew racing to the convenience store to buy some. She was nervous that he wouldn't make it back in time, and she was right to be nervous. At five-to-seven, the doorbell rang. Wiping her hands on a towel, she headed for the front door, little Lacy screaming her excitement as she followed along. Tricia would have screamed as well if she wasn't so nervous and ready to throw up.

When she opened the door, Landon stood there, smiling as he held a bottle of merlot. "I know you said not to bring anything, but who shows up to a dinner party empty-handed?" He offered her the bottle, and she took it gesturing for him to come in, telling Lacy to go check on her brother.

"Drew will be back shortly," she said as she led Landon into the kitchen. "I ran out of butter, and you have to have butter with baked potatoes."

"A must for sure," Landon said, still smiling as he leaned back on the counter, arms over his chest. He glanced at the door as if checking to see if the kids were heading into the kitchen. "I enjoyed the basketball game today," he said. "Thanks for letting me join in the family fun."

She felt the heat rush up her neck as she remembered how well he had enjoyed the game as he held her when she almost hit the concrete. "My pleasure. It was fun having you join us." She felt her heart start to race, the pounding in her ears. "Thanks for keeping me from busting my ass."

His grin grew. "Well, it was too nice of an ass to have scuffed up with scratch marks."

She blushed, staring at him, shocked that he was so brazen, yet loving it at the same time. She liked bold even though she had never had bold before. "Well, my ass appreciates it, I assure you." She pulled a corkscrew out of a drawer and handed it toward him. "You can open that wine and pour us each a glass. Unless, of course, you want a beer instead."

Landon reached out to take the corkscrew, his fingers grazing hers. That touch silenced her for a moment as it sent electrical tremors throughout her body. He just grinned at her as he pulled the corkscrew out of her hand. "Wine will be fine, thanks."

She swallowed as she nodded, her voice lost to the passion that thrummed between her legs. With a deep breath, she forced the words to pass her lips. "Great. Glasses are in that cabinet behind you." She could feel the fluttering in her chest as she remembered the way he felt when he held her in the driveway earlier that day, his cock pressing against her.

"I'm not making you uncomfortable, am I?" he asked as she turned back to finish fixing the salad for dinner.

Uncomfortable was not the right word. "I'm fine, really," she said. "Although, I must admit to being in a place I've never been before, feeling things I've never felt." She felt the blush ride up her neck with her confession.

He grinned as he started to twist the corkscrew down into the bottle. "And what exactly are you feeling?" His smirk told her he knew exactly what she felt. He just wanted to hear her say it.

She took a deep breath. Should she even cross this line? She had never cheated on Drew before, and never really thought she ever would, but god, she couldn't get this man out of her mind. "Conflicted, and horny as hell," she finally said, and he just grinned as he poured the wine. She turned to him, dropping her hands to the counter, lettuce in her hands. "I've never felt like this before. I don't cheat on my husband."

Landon arched an eyebrow at her as he smirked. "You haven't cheated on your husband. Yet." He winked at her, and it sent a shiver through her body that settled between her legs.

"It's that yet part that is driving me crazy," she said, turning her attention back to the salad she was preparing. She had probably said too much, but Landon was right. She hadn't cheated on Drew yet, and there was still time to keep it from happening. All she had to do was keep her legs closed. She gave a silent sigh. That was her problem. She didn't want to keep her legs closed. She wanted to spread them wide open and wrap them around Landon's waist as he drove his cock into her.

At that moment, Drew called out that he was back, and Lacy squealed from the bedroom. Tricia gave a silent thank you that the subject had to be changed, unsure where it would have gone if they had continued.

Drew leaned in and kissed her cheek once he walked into the

kitchen, the bag with the butter in hand. He then shook Landon's hand as he set the bag on the counter. Glancing over at Tricia, he asked, "Ready for me to get the grill started? Time to heat some things up."

Tricia felt the blush hit her cheeks as the heat pooled in the valley between her legs. Things had already been pretty heated up.

SEVEN

Bradley was in daycare, Lacy was at school, and Drew was finally on his way to work. Tricia sighed, ready to enjoy a quiet Monday all to herself, and she knew the first thing she wanted to do. She headed straight for her nightstand and the vibrator she knew waited for her urgent needs. However, before she could make it to the hallway, a noise outside caught her attention, drawing her to the front window. There, across the street, was Landon Turner shutting his car door as he slid out from behind the steering wheel. Confusion bunched her brows up over her nose. *Shouldn't he be in school?*

Before she could think better of her decision, she opened her front door, stepping out into the morning chill. "Playing hookie?" she asked, hands on her hips as she grinned over at him. "Someone needs a detention. Or better yet, a paddling."

He chuckled as he started walking toward her, shaking his head. "I'm the teacher. I send people to detention, and I'm the one who does the paddling. I think I'm safe."

"Oh, is that right? And what does it take to get sent to your detention?" Tricia bit her bottom lip, amazed that she was pushing his buttons after their dinner Saturday night, but unable to stop herself. She wouldn't mind getting a spanking from this man strolling toward her, his gait cocky and sure.

He smirked as he raked her with his gaze. "Why be a naughty girl, of course." He then cocked his head at her. "And how about you, Tricia? Are you a naughty girl? Do you need to be sent to detention?"

She bit her lower lip as the war raged within her. She had opened the door, and damn it if Landon hadn't walked right through it. Now, did she follow through on the game before her or turn around and leave him standing there? With a deep breath, and a burning in her pussy, she made her decision. "Oh, Mr. Turner, I'm a very naughty girl," she said. "I need you to show me the error of my ways."

He grinned, the lust obvious in his eyes. "Oh, it'll be my pleasure, little girl." He grabbed her by the hand and led her across the street back toward his house. Tricia's eyes popped open wide as she jerked her attention around to see if her neighbors were watching. She didn't need someone telling Drew they saw his cheating wife being dragged across the street to Landon's house.

Still, her cunt dripped at the thought of being seen. God, she was a mixture of emotions and desires.

Once Landon had her in his own home, he spun her around, gripping her by the waist and pressing her tight against him. "You are a naughty little girl, aren't you?" But before she could answer, he pressed his lips to hers, his warm, firm lips, as he kissed her with a hunger that melted her pussy into a puddle of passion. Heat flared through her as she surrendered to his embrace, wrapping her hands around his back and pressing into him tighter, her breasts pushing up against them. She felt his hands slipping up into her hair, taking a fistful as he slipped his tongue into her mouth, tasting her. She groaned, falling into him more.

When he broke the kiss, he kept a handful of her hair as he stared deeply into her eyes, grinning. "Are you ready for your paddling?" His voice was heavy with the lust that filled both of them.

"Yes, Mr. Turner," she replied, her voice soft, timid. She wasn't sure she actually wanted him to spank her since she had never been punished that way before, not even as a child. Yet, she wasn't about to deny this man anything right then.

He led her over to the couch, sitting down while he left her standing. He glanced up into her eyes as he said, "Last chance to change your mind, Tricia."

"I'm not changing my mind, Mr. Turner. I'm yours to do with as you please."

He nodded, that grin of his still plastered on his face. He reached up and grabbed her shorts, and she sucked in a breath as his fingers grazed her waist. Keeping his eyes on her, he pulled the shorts down her legs, taking her thong with him, baring her most private of parts to his gaze. Only when her shorts were down around her knees did he look down her body at the treasure he had uncovered. She watched as he leaned over, his nose almost touching her pussy, and inhaled the scent of her. When he leaned back, he said, "I'm going to enjoy taking that." Then his grin turned mischievous. "But first..." With a sudden pull, she was bent over his lap, ass up in the air. He pulled her shirt over her breasts and quickly unclasped her bra, shoving it up and out of the way as well, her tits hanging free. "Now, for being a naughty girl, I think you should feel the sting of my hand. Are you a naughty girl?"

"Yes!" She took a deep breath. "Yes, Mr. Turner. I'm a very naughty girl."

"And how are you naughty?" She felt his hand caressing her ass, gliding over her round cheeks bringing a pleasant shiver to her body.

"Because I'm here with you, a married woman, and all I can think about is how your cock will feel driving into my wet pussy."

There was no warning as he smacked her ass, the sting shooting through her. She cried out, the pain lingering as it sent a flame to her clitoris, making her pearl throb. Then another. And another. A fire started in her ass with each smack of his hand. "Yes, a very naughty girl," he said. "And I can't wait to give you what you deserve." He spanked her again, and she felt herself squirming on his lap with each smack. She also felt his cock growing harder, and it made her shove her ass up to meet each one of his slaps to her ass. She cried out, begging for him to punish her, to give her what she deserved.

He smacked her ass again, and with his other hand, he reached down and started toying with her nipple, twisting it in tight circles as he spanked her sweet ass, her body shaking, squirming, as she cried out, the pain of his attention sending pleasure coursing throughout her body to pool between her legs. "Oh, god, more. Please, Mr. Landon, give me more." She had never been spanked before, and now, she wanted to be spanked by this man all the time.

After he smacked her ass a few more times, her rear on fire to the point she knew he left handprints she would not be able to explain to her husband later that night, he held her by the arm and plopped her down onto her knees. She stared up at him as he stood, his hands going to his pants button, his gaze fixed on her. As he undid his pants and slid them down his legs, his cock sprang into sight, long and thick, and she felt her pussy gush at the sight. She had to have that monster inside of her.

"And is my naughty little girl ready for the rest of her punishment?" he asked.

She licked her lips as she stared at his cock, nodding her head.

EIGHT

Landon shed himself of his shoes and pants, and then sat back down on the couch, his legs spread. He crooked his finger at her, calling her to kneel in front of him. She quickly obeyed, her heart pounding in her ears as she yearned for his massive cock. "Are you ready to be a good little girl?" he asked as he reached out and gripped her hair in a tight fist, pulling her mouth to his cock.

Tricia took a deep breath as she nodded. "Yes, Mr. Landon. I plan on being a *very* good girl." She licked her lips and then lowered her head down to Landon's throbbing cock. She twirled her tongue around the velvety head, tasting the pre-cum from the tip, allowing it to glide across her tongue as she lapped it into her mouth. With a tight grip on her hair, Landon forced his cock into her mouth, fucking her face as he shoved her up and down on his hard shaft. Tricia groaned as she took his cock, his dark curls touching her nose as he continued to slide her mouth up and down the length of his hardness.

"That's a good girl," he said. "Show me how good of a student you are for your teacher." He gripped her hair tighter as she swallowed his shaft, loving the feel of every vein and the ridge of the head of his cock as she swallowed it. She could feel it throbbing in her mouth as she reached out and gripped the bottom of his cock with one hand and his thigh with the other to brace herself. He spread his legs wider for her as she scooted closer for comfort, her head bobbing up and down his length. She couldn't wait to feel his manhood inside of her, stretching her pussy the way it was stretching her mouth.

She could feel the juices dripping from her sex, her wetness coating her folds as her pussy yearned to be stuffed with Landon's cock. Yet, he had other plans.

Pulling her mouth from his rod, he lifted her until she was sitting on the couch as he slid to his knees on the floor. He lifted her legs, draping them over his shoulders as he cupped the underside of her thighs. "I think that deserves a little bit of a reward," he said.

Tricia watched as he lowered his mouth to her pussy, felt his tongue glide up her slit until it found her precious pearl at the top, hard and throbbing. He pushed on it with his tongue pressed flat, licking it and then flicking his tongue over it, sending electrical charges through her body as she gripped the couch with her fists.

"Oh god, Mr. Turner, more, please more." She squirmed on his face as he tongued her pussy, licking up one side of her folds and then down the other before shoving his tongue into her wet hole, fucking her, tasting her. She reached down and gripped his head, forcing his mouth harder onto her cunt as she ground against his tongue. "Yes! Oh god, yes!" She clutched her eyes shut as she surrendered to Landon's machinations, giving herself over to whatever he wanted to do to her.

Landon kept sucking on her pussy as he shoved two fingers into her dripping honey, pumping them in and out. As his tongue glided over her clit, he crooked his finger, rubbing it against that sweet spot at the top of her cunt, pressing it hard against her wall and sending tremors of ecstasy shooting through her. He pounded into her, his knuckles hitting her folds as he squeezed her thigh with his other hand. This was the ultimate pleasure. Her entire body vibrated in response to his tongue on her pussy. Her eyes popped open as she felt her orgasm building within her, her body tightening into a knot that was ready to rip apart. Then, just as she thought she was about to explode, her orgasm rocketed through her, her body shuddering as she rolled her head side-to-side, crying out, her back arching as she pressed her shoulders into the back of the couch. "Yes! Yes! Don't stop!"

Landon didn't stop until her body settled on the couch, her chest heaving with her breathing as her orgasm subsided. When she had collapsed into the cushion, he leaned back, her juices coating his lips and chin. With a waggle of his eyebrows, he said, "Don't rest yet, little girl. It's time for you to satisfy your teacher now."

With a grin, he grabbed her by the arm and pulled her up off the couch and down onto her knees, spinning her so that she faced the couch. With a hand in the middle of her back, he bent her over and kneed her legs open, her ass pointing up into the air. He smacked her rump again as he pulled her backward a little with his other hand, putting her exactly where he wanted her. "Are you ready for it?" he asked. "Do you want my cock, you naughty little housewife?"

"Yes, oh god, yes!" She shoved her ass back trying to shove his cock into her pink slit.

Landon held her back from her goal, however. "That's a good girl. Beg for it. Beg for my cock like a good little girl."

"Please, Mr. Turner, I need it," she pleaded with him. "Please, fuck me. Give me your cock. Use my married pussy. Please, teach me your lesson."

Landon gripped her hips as he growled. With one thrust, he buried himself inside of her pussy, sinking his cock into her until his balls slapped her clit, making her cry out as she shoved herself back onto his meaty shaft.

NINE

Tricia shoved herself back onto Landon's cock, relishing the way he spread her pussy around his massive shaft. He gripped her hips, his fingers digging into her flesh as he pulled her back and forth on his meaty rod. She cried out, small mewling noises mixed with her pleading passion. "Fuck me, Mr. Turner! Punish my pussy. Please!" He drove into her harder, faster, pounding her ass with his hips as he pummeled her soaking cunt.

She could hear him grunting behind her, could hear his heavy breathing as his cock throbbed within her. There were no thoughts of Drew, or how wrong the act she was committing was. All she thought about was how great Landon's cock felt buried between her bald folds, her pussy walls sucking his shaft as he speared her with it. "That's a good girl," she heard him say. "Take your teacher's cock. Such a good little slut for teacher." He kept pounding into her, and she felt the cresting wave of her orgasm start to build as she shoved herself back onto his cock, felt her body tighten and start to shudder as she cried out, relishing the feeling coursing through her right then. His cock felt amazing in her pussy, long and thick, touching places that had not been touched before. She kept bouncing back on his manhood, trying to get even more of his meaty shaft deeper inside of her. She arched her back as her orgasm broke, crashing down on her body and spreading out through her limbs and nerves. She froze, pinning herself onto his cock as her body was washed with the warmth of her climax filling her, her mouth popping open as a silent scream left her.

Landon dug his fingers into her, his hands gripping her tight against him as she jerked on his cock. She could feel his manhood throb and twitch and knew she was about to feel his passion filling her. She wanted his cum, even though she knew she shouldn't let him fill her, not being on birth control. Still, she didn't care. She wanted to feel it, feel his hot seed fill her womb. He grunted, digging his fingers into her harder, and then his cum exploded from his cock, spraying her inner walls and filling her married pussy. Their bodies froze together as their orgasms struck and then subsided, leaving them panting and sweaty.

When Tricia's orgasm finally vanished, she fell forward on the couch, feeling his cock slip from her soaked pussy as she did, her mind groaning at the loss. Yet, she still felt him deep inside of her from where he had just fucked her, her knees sore from being slid on the carpet. How she would explain that to Drew, she didn't know, nor did she care. All she cared about was how great she felt, how great her body felt, after having Landon's—Mr. Turner's—cock buried balls deep into her. She was already missing being filled with him.

She felt his hands on her as he slowly turned her, helping her to sit on the floor. He slid around until he sat beside her, his arm draped around her shoulders. They were both still breathing pretty heavy as she laid her head on his shoulder.

"So, how did you like my detention?" he asked, and she could hear the grin in his voice.

She felt herself grinning as well. "You can keep me after class anytime," she replied.

"That naughty of a little girl, are you?" He squeezed her shoulders.

"With you, I think I'm going to be very naughty." She settled in against him as she felt their juices slip from her pussy, her folds still swollen from the pounding he just gave her. She knew this wasn't a onetime fling. She had his cock and wanted more of it. She was ready to be Mr. Turner's naughty girl anytime he wanted.

"Well, good thing I have the rest of the day off, isn't it?" he said.

She slid a hand down his stomach to grip his cock, which was still at half-mast. "Oh, definitely. Most definitely." She grinned and then lowered her head to his manhood once again.

CUCKOLDED BY THE NEIGHBORS

ONE

"It'll be fun," Jenny said as she started putting together a small bag of goodies to take over to their neighbors. "Mark and Brenda have been trying to get us to come hang out with them for weeks, and it's the perfect day for it. Mark's even offered to grill while we lay out and enjoy the pool. They even have a full bar to help us relax. What's there not to like?"

Brian groaned inwardly. There was plenty not to like in his mind, the first of which was how he had noticed his wife staring at Mark's broader shoulders and more powerful frame. He hadn't missed how the two of them had smiled back and forth at each other when talking or how Jenny always seemed to stand so close to Mark whenever they were around each other, touching him when she giggled at one of his jokes. She never giggled at Brian's jokes. That Jenny was infatuated with their neighbor was quite obvious, and Mark didn't hide the fact that he welcomed her attention, not even when his own wife was around. "And now you're going to wear that skimpy bathing suit over there for him to ogle your body," Brian continued his whining. "I just think it's a little too much friendliness between neighbors."

Jenny rolled her eyes as she turned around to face him, the fabric of her bathing suit top barely covering her ample breasts, her nipples already straining against the flimsy material. "You really do have too much imagination," she said. "Of course, I think he's good looking—damn good looking, actually—but that doesn't mean I'd ever do anything without your permission." She gave him a wink before turning back around to finish loading the bag.

He stopped what he was doing and stared at her slender back, soaking in her scantily clad ass that he just knew Mark was going to be trying to grab all afternoon. "Without my permission?" He couldn't believe what he heard. Was she actually thinking of having sex with their neighbor? "Don't you think that just proves my point about this being a bad idea?"

She shook her head, not turning around to face him. "No. All I think it proves is that you're a little paranoid. Now, be a good boy and go get your bathing suit on." She glanced over her shoulder at him and smirked with a bounce of her eyebrows.

"Good boy? You're enjoying this a little too much already." Still, he left the kitchen to carry out her orders, thinking this whole afternoon was a giant mistake and wishing he had the guts to call the entire thing off. His stomach was a mass of knots as he slipped out of his pants and moved to fetch his bathing suit, images of how Mark and Jenny touched each other when they talked floating through his head. Nothing overtly sexual, which was probably the problem. No, it was more casual caresses on the arm as she laughed at one of Mark's jokes or the lingering hug when they greeted each other, the friendly peck on the cheek a little too friendly.

As he slid his bathing suit up his legs, Brian had to tuck his hardening cock to the side to get it inside, his growing manhood contradicting his inward jealousy, which frustrated him even more. The idea of seeing his wife with another man had always turned him on, but not their neighbor, and not in reality. It was a fantasy, something for him to jerk off to when she had one of her constant headaches. Brian bet she'd never have a headache with Mark.

He touched his cock before pulling his bathing suit all the way up, stroking it to even fuller life as he thought of his wife down on her knees in front of another man, sucking his cock to life, her giant tits swaying as…

"Stop touching your dick, Brian, and get your ass out here so we can go," Jenny called from the kitchen, making Brian jump as if she had walked in on him and caught him masturbating. Jenny didn't know he jacked off to images of her with others, didn't know he jacked off period.

Did she?

He finished putting on his bathing suit, slipped on a T-shirt, and headed out of the bedroom. When he reached the kitchen, Jenny stood there in her skimpy bikini, the bag of snacks in one hand and a beach towel in the other. He just stared at her a moment, his eyes wide as he soaked in her practically naked body. "Aren't you going to wear one of your cover-ups?"

Jenny laughed. "And why would I do that? I'm just going to be taking it off once I get there. I can't exactly go swimming or enjoy the sun if I'm wearing a cover-up."

"But what about the other neighbors?" he asked, still astonished that she would walk around outside with most of her body exposed, especially her ass and tits. "Are you planning on giving everyone a free show?"

She grinned as she walked past him, wiggling her ass as she did. "If you got it, flaunt it, right?" She winked at him as she passed him. "Now, let's go get into some trouble."

He groaned again as he watched her walk to the front door, sashaying her ass for dramatic effect. He really hoped old man Harrison wasn't in his front yard cutting grass right then.

TWO

Of course, Old Man Harrison *was* out in his front yard when they walked across their lawn, and he didn't hesitate to stop and stare at Jenny as she sashayed across their front lawn to the Bennetts. Brian just glared at the old man as he followed his wife.

Old Man Harrison just shrugged as if to say who could blame him for looking.

Brian continued to follow Jenny toward the Bennetts front door, still thinking this was a bad idea, but unable to call it off without appearing to be a total dick. When they reached the front door, Jenny stepped to the side and gestured for him to knock. He sighed, but did as she wanted, knocking twice on the hardwood door, hoping the Bennets forgot they had invited them over and were gone. He wasn't so lucky, however, and a few seconds after he knocked, Mark opened the door, his large dark frame intimidating to Brian but an aphrodisiac to Jenny as the man stood there in nothing but his bathing suit.

"Hey, neighbors," Mark said as he gestured for them to enter his home. "Glad you made it. Brenda and I have wanted to have the two of you over for quite some time."

Jenny flowed past Brian, smiling as she reached out and touched Mark's bare chest as she passed him. "I agree," she said. "We should have done this a long time ago."

Brian worried about knowing what *this* was in his wife's mind. "Hey, Mark," he said, trying his best to sound calm in the throes of his jealousy. "Thanks for having us over."

Mark patted Brian's back after he shut the door and started to guide them through the front of the house toward the kitchen. "My pleasure. What kind of neighbors would we be if we didn't share the good times?"

The kind who didn't stare at my wife, Brian thought as he followed the others through the house.

When they reached the kitchen, Brenda was putting the finishing touches on a pasta salad, standing by the kitchen counter in her bikini, which was just as skimpy as Jenny's if not more so. Brian tried hard not to stare, but found it difficult as Brenda's dark ass cheeks hung out both sides of her skimpy bottoms, the fabric practically swallowed by her ass crack, calling his eyes to stare. When she turned to greet them, her large breasts oozed over the sides of her top, which barely covered her hard nipples. She was gorgeous, a black goddess, and Brian wondered why Mark would flirt with Jenny when he had Brenda to come home to every night.

"Hey, neighbors," Brenda squealed as she left what she was doing to give Brian and Jenny both hugs, lingering on Jenny almost as long as Mark usually did. "I'm so glad you're here."

"God, Brenda, you look amazing," Jenny said as she held the other woman out at arms' length and gawked at her body. "I love that bathing suit."

"Oh, please," Brenda said, waving off the compliment. "To be honest, it took me forever to find it. Being just the two of us here, we hardly ever use bathing suits. The sun feels so good on my skin. I almost had to wear an old shorts outfit today until I found this thing in the back of one of my drawers."

"With that body, I'm sure you would have looked sexy in anything," Jenny said. "Of course, if you had told us skinny dipping was an option...." She giggled as she set the bag of snacks she brought on the kitchen table.

Mark laughed. "Skinny dipping is always an option."

Brian just smiled, forcing a small laugh past his lips. He didn't want to seem prudish, but his gut twisted at the thought of Mark being naked around Jenny. The man's cock was visible enough from the outline in his bathing suit, and from what Brian could see, Mark's manhood made his look like he hadn't reached puberty, yet.

"How about we get this party started?" Mark suggested. "I

have a cooler of beer already out by the pool and a pitcher of margaritas just waiting to be guzzled. It's too beautiful of a day to miss standing around a boring old kitchen."

"Agreed," Brenda said as she picked up a vegetable tray from the counter and headed for the back door.

"I'm game," Jenny added as she started to follow Brenda out the sliding glass doors to the back patio.

Brian forced himself to smile as he nodded. "A beer sounds great." Maybe it would help cool down the jealousy he felt right then.

The Bennetts' backyard was an oasis from the real world with a grill and bar set off to the south of the pool, chaise lounge chairs along the decking, and even a concrete table with benches in the shallow end of the pool. A round table with chairs and an umbrella sat next to the grill, and that's where Brenda carried the tray of snacks while Mark went behind the bar to get everyone their drinks.

Jenny placed their towels on a lounge chair and sauntered up to the bar. "Wow," she said. "Your place looks amazing. I'm surprised we ever see you out front. I think I'd live back here."

Mark chuckled as he poured the ladies margaritas. "Your home should be a sanctuary from the world," he said. "Make it so that you'd rather be there than anywhere else is my motto."

Brian sat in one of the chairs around the table as Brenda uncovered the vegetable tray. "I'd say you've done an awesome job of that," he said. "As Jenny said, I'd live out here. And your privacy fence is high enough to give you complete isolation."

"Although, now that I know you both go without bathing suits, I may have to peek over the fence more often," Jenny said, grinning.

Mark glanced at her, his face a mask of lusty hunger. "Peek over anytime," he said. "See anything you like, then feel free to climb the fence and join." He winked at her, and Brian felt the knot in his stomach grow tighter.

THREE

"I'm ready for one of those margaritas," Brenda said as she moved over to the bar, standing real close to Jenny, Brian noticed. "This heat makes me extra thirsty."

Jenny leaned on the bar, her tits almost falling out of her bathing suit as she watched Mark fix their drinks. It was quite obvious Mark noticed. The funny part to Brian was that Brenda seemed to notice as well and didn't seem at all upset by Jenny's display or her husband's frank approval. Brian expected their neighbor to be jealous over his wife's obvious attention to Mark, but Brenda seemed to take it all in stride as if nothing unusual was happening in front of her.

With drinks in hand, they all ventured over to the pool, sliding down into the sun-warm water one step at a time. Brian noticed Jenny moved to lean against the wall, and that Mark moved closer to her while Brenda moved to the other side of Brian, leaving Brian and Mark standing beside each other. At first, he thought it odd, that the women would flank the men, and that the men weren't standing beside their own wives. Still, it was a small get-together and a very large pool. He would force his insecurities down and focus on relaxing and having fun. He would. At least, he thought he would until he noticed Jenny staring at Mark's crotch, a smile curving the corners of her lips upward.

Glancing in the same direction, Brian couldn't help but stare as well. With Mark's bathing suit now wet, the material hugged the man's cock—his massive cock. The thing had to be at least ten inches long and more than three inches thick. How in the hell could anyone take a monster like that into their cunts?

"Isn't it something, Jenny?" Brenda asked as she slid closer to Brian, her eyes watching Jenny gawk at how big Mark's manhood was even limp.

Jenny glanced away, her cheeks turning red, embarrassed from being so blatantly caught, Brian assumed. "I'm sorry," she stammered, moving a little away from Mark. Brian also noticed she didn't move *that* far away from Mark. "I've just never seen a cock that big before. Brian's is so small compared to Mark's. I shouldn't have been staring, though."

"Jenny!" Brian shouted, more so because of the embarrassment of being called small in front of their neighbors than her open admission of staring at Mark's shaft.

"Oh, don't be embarrassed, sweetie," Brenda said as she moved past Brian to get closer to Jenny. "Not many white women see a cock this big. You should take advantage of it while you can. Trust me, I don't mind. I get plenty of Mark's massive rod whenever I want him, and he sure loves pounding into a white woman's pussy. Says it always feels so tight because it's hardly ever been stretched like a pussy should."

Brian just stood and watched as Brenda practically gave Jenny permission to check out her husband's cock. *What the hell is going on here?*

"You really don't mind?" Jenny asked without ever taking her eyes off Mark's crotch. Brian could see the man's cock getting harder inside of his bathing suit from the attention Jenny was giving him, and she hadn't even touched him yet.

"By all means," Brenda said. "Brian's cock isn't even making a bump in his suit; I can only imagine how deprived for a real cock you've been. Mark can show you anything you want to see." Brenda slid over beside Brian again, but this time she was between him and her husband, her attention solely on Jenny and Mark, almost blocking Brian from watching. "Don't by shy, sweetie. Explore that monster."

Brian was about to say something, say how his wife wouldn't do it, wouldn't touch another man's cock, but stopped, his mouth open, as Jenny slid through the water to get closer to Mark. Brian watched as his petite wife reached out and took the strings to

Mark's bathing suit in her hands, pulling them loose. She didn't even look into Mark's face, but rather kept staring at the cock she was about to reveal. Inwardly, Brian begged his wife to stop before she went too far, but Jenny showed no intention of stopping. He watched as under the surface of the water, Jenny pulled Mark's bathing suit wide open, the man's hard cock popping into sight. Jenny released the bathing suit, wrapping her hand around Mark's manhood and stroking it, her mouth slightly open, her tongue appearing along her bottom lip.

"That's right, honey," Brenda said. "Feel what a real cock feels like. That's what a woman needs fucked with, not some tiny little nub of a cock that just leaves us wanting more." Brenda turned and glanced at Brian, a smirk across her face. "She may never touch your little dick again once she has a taste of a real man."

Brian opened his mouth to say something, but his words were cut off by his wife's mesmerized words. "I want it in my mouth." Her gaze fixated on the massive rod in her hands. "Can I? Please?"

Mark moved over to the side of the pool, sliding up as his bathing suit floated down his legs and off as he walked. Naked, he sat on the edge of the pool, his legs dangling in the water as his cock stood tall and proud. Brian could only watch as Jenny slid through the water toward their neighbor's cock, forgetting that Brian was even there, forgetting that she promised she wouldn't do anything without his permission. It was almost like Mark's cock hypnotized her, calling her to it.

Mark had yet to say anything, just stood there—now sat there—and allowed Jenny to grope him while his wife watched. Now, Mark just glanced down at Jenny, his lips curved up in a grin of invitation.

Jenny gripped Mark's cock again as she stood between his legs, his cock even with her breasts before she leaned down and ran her tongue over the head of his cock. Brian almost groaned out loud as he watched his wife swallow their neighbor's massive cock, her hand running up and down his hardness as she sucked him off. Mark looked over Jenny's head at Brian, another smirk on his lips, but this one for a whole other reason. Brian just felt the knot in his stomach twist again as his cock twitched to life.

FOUR

Brian watched as Jenny's head bobbed up and down, Mark's hand on her head, guiding her as he watched her enjoy his thick cock.

"Look at how your wife is devouring Mark's cock," Brenda said as she leaned up against Brian. He felt her hand slide down his stomach to his cock, rubbing his hard member through his bathing suit. "You want to tell me you hate it, but your body doesn't lie, and from what I'm feeling, she'll love having my husband's long, thick, black cock buried inside of her. We'll have to find another use for you, won't we?" She gripped his cock, squeezing it hard. "Get out of your bathing suit and get your little ass up by those chairs." She then turned and moved to the stairs as she untied her bathing suit top, letting it fall to the pool's surface as she walked.

Brian could only stare as her dark, ample breasts came into full view, her hard nipples tiny buds in the middle of her dark aureoles. He glanced back over his shoulder and watched as Mark slid down into the water, pushing Jenny against the wall, her tits sliding along the tile as he pulled her ass out a little. Mark stepped behind Jenny, his hands on her waist as his cock slid up and down her ass crack.

"Come here, my little boy," Brenda said as she stretched an arm out, her fingers wiggling for him to come to her. She had already stripped out of her bikini bottoms, her legs open so that Brian had a great view of her bald pussy. "Come sit beside me and watch as your wife gets fucked for the first time. She'll feel like a virgin compared to what she's used to being fucked with."

Brian obeyed without question, sitting down on the chair beside Brenda as he turned his gaze to his wife. Mark had his hands on Jenny's hips as he growled into her ears. "Are you ready for a real man? Do you want this cock?"

"Please!" Jenny screamed as she looked back at Mark over her shoulder. "Fuck me. I want your cock. Give it to me!"

Brian felt the twist in his stomach as he watched his wife beg for another man's cock, a much larger cock. He felt Brenda's hand toying with his cock, stroking it as they watched Mark drive his monster into Jenny. She only used two fingers to stroke him, and Jenny had to use her entire hand to grip Mark's cock, and her fingers hadn't even closed around his shaft.

Jenny pushed her ass back as she continued to beg Mark to take her, no longer caring that she begged for another man's cock in front of her husband. Mark gripped her hips tighter as he thrust his cock all the way inside of her cunt, making her gasp as she clawed at the side of the pool. "God, yes!" Jenny screamed. "So fucking big; your cock is so fucking big. God, you're splitting me open."

Brian felt his stomach churn at her words. She had never screamed out like this when he fucked her. Would she ever want his cock again?

"See?" Brenda asked him. "That's how a woman reacts when a real man fucks her. Now, get your little white ass down between my legs and start licking my pussy. The only thing we need you for now is your mouth. Your cock is useless."

Brian scampered off the chair, kneeling at the end as he leaned over the bottom of the chair, burying his face between Brenda's dark legs as she shoved his face down toward her pussy, which glistened with her wetness. As he slid his tongue up between her folds, he heard his wife screaming out, begging for Mark to fuck her harder. Brenda put her hands on his head, holding his mouth to her pussy as she slid her cunt up and down on his mouth, grinding against him.

"That's it, boy, hear your wife begging for my husband's cock," Brenda taunted him, her thighs clamped around his head as she held his face to her pussy. "She'll never want that tiny dick of yours again after having a real cock in her pussy. Oh, but don't you worry. There will be plenty for your mouth to do. You do have a talented tongue." She ground her cunt up and down on his face to the point Brian thought he would suffocate. "Keep licking!" she snapped. "Don't you dare stop licking my pussy, boy, or I'll spank your ass good and hard in front of your wife. You're my little bitch now, and I'll use you as often as I need. Your cute little wife will be busy serving my husband's cock. She's a real black cock whore now."

Brian felt his cock twitch at everything Brenda said to him as he lapped at her pussy and the shame of it burned his cheeks. Still, he couldn't deny how turned on it made him to know that Jenny would be Mark's toy while he served Brenda. His life, especially his sex life, would never be the same now that his wife had felt a real cock between her legs.

Brenda cried out as she clamped her thighs around his head even harder, her legs shaking as she pressed his mouth even tighter onto her pussy, her orgasm flooding through her. Brian continued to lick at her pussy as he held her thighs, his tongue gliding over her swollen clit as she held his head in place. It didn't take long before her climax subsided, and she released his head, smiling down at him. "Yes, we will definitely make good use of that tongue of yours," she said as she ran her tongue over her lips. "Now, get your ass up here. I want to see you stroke that little dick of yours while my husband finishes claiming your wife."

Brian didn't say anything, happy to at least be offered some form of release. Quickly, he scampered up until he sat on the edge of Brenda's chair, his ass half hanging off as she wrapped an arm around him. She touched his hard cock, giggling. "Such a sad excuse for a dick."

Brian only nodded, knowing she was right.

FIVE

As soon as Brian balanced himself beside Brenda on her chair, she gave him permission to stroke his pitiful excuse for a dick. He needed no further urging, his cock throbbing from what Brenda forced him to endure and the sounds of his wife being fucked coming from the pool. As his gaze landed on his wife and Mark, the giant black man having her bent over on the pool steps as he stood behind her and pounded into her, Brian couldn't help but notice how thick Mark's cock was. Brian barely needed two fingers to jack himself off, and it would take Jenny's entire hand on Mark's cock, and Brian doubted she would be able to close her fingers. Jenny's face was a mask of pure pleasure as Mark dug his fingers into her hips and shoved his monster shaft in and out of her wet cunt. At one point, Jenny opened her eyes, looking at Brian, but he doubted she even saw him, lost in Mark's cock as she was.

"God, Mark, you're so fucking big," she groaned. "I've never been so full."

Brian felt the twisting in his stomach as his cock throbbed even more, hating what he heard, but unable to deny how it made his cock hard.

"Oh, god," Jenny shrieked. "Mark, don't stop. Oh, god, I'm...I'm...Oh, god, I'm coming!" Brian watched as his petite wife shoved herself back onto mark's giant spear, impaling her pussy onto him as her body shook with the strongest orgasm he had ever witnessed her having, and it wasn't him who gave it to her. He doubted he would ever be able to make her come after this. She wouldn't want his miserable little dick as Brenda said.

As Jenny's body shook, Brian heard Mark grunt as he pulled her back, holding her in place on his cock, and Brian knew the man was coming inside of Jenny without protection of any kind. Jenny didn't even seem to care as she rode the wave of her climax, Mark keeping her from slipping from the pool steps. When their orgasms subsided, Mark spun Jenny around to face him, his powerful hands going to her back as he pressed the smaller woman against him and kissed her hard. Jenny just hung on him as she surrendered to the kiss.

When they broke the kiss, Jenny looked over at Brian, and the way she stared at him, stroking his dick with two fingers, was all it took to cause him to shoot his load all over his chest. He grunted and then Brenda laughed at him. "Is that all you had? Two small strands of cum? I bet there's a gallon inside your pretty wife there. No wonder she eagerly took every drop."

Brian felt his face flush with shame as he stared at Jenny who only joined in the laughter.

"Now, you clean that shit up so we can get back to the cooking," Brenda ordered.

Brian moved to obey her, but she stopped him with a shake of her head. "You're not wasting a towel on such a little amount. Lick it up. Right now."

Brian felt his cheeks burn hotter, but he dared not refuse the woman. As he tried not to watch Jenny, he lifted his hand to his mouth and sucked his own cum from his fingers. He then swiped the white gunk from his chest and stomach and swallowed it as well.

"Well, I never would have believed it," Jenny said. "He's a little cum eater. This will be fun."

Brian finally looked up and saw Jenny and Mark walking toward them, water dripping from their naked bodies as Mark had his arm around Jenny's waist, keeping her pressed to him as they walked, claiming her in front of her husband. Brian knew there was nothing he could do about it. Jenny had found the cock she craved, and he would just have to deal with it, enduring the humiliation that she preferred another man to her own husband.

"Oh, believe it, sweetie," Brenda said as she pushed Brian off her chair and rose to her feet. "You'll discover this husband of yours has other uses besides disappointing you with that tiny dick of his. I'll be more than happy to show you while Mark gives you a good pounding. I know you don't want to give up his cock after you felt it in your tight pussy."

"Oh, I don't think I could," Jenny said as she glanced down at Mark's flaccid member, which still looked three times bigger than Brian's hard cock. She then turned to Brenda. "As long as you don't mind sharing, that is."

"Oh, I'll have your hubby here keeping me satisfied," Brenda said. "I have plenty of uses for a white man with a tiny dick." She patted Brian's chest. "We'll have plenty of fun, won't we?"

Brian just nodded his head, a lump in his throat keeping him from saying anything. He watched as Mark slid his hand into Jenny's, their fingers intertwined as they walked over to the grill. Brenda swatted Brian's ass, ordering him to fix them all drinks. "Yes, ma'am," he said, weakly, knowing his role in all their lives had just changed, and his cock throbbed at the thought.

Avery Rowan's Books

On Amazon

Exploration while Camping
Served Picnic Style
Taken in the Woods
Taken by the Fire
Her Swimming Holes
Taken While Camping Box Set

Adventures in Swinging
Venturing Out
Play Date
After Party
Chelsea's Date
House Party
Darren's Surprise
Swinging Neighbors
Swinging Vacation

Cuckold Stories
From the Front Seat
His Booty-Call Wife
Housewife's Revenge
Cuckolded By The Neighbors
Cuckolded By Her Ex

Cuckolded by a Stranger

<u>*The Cuckolding of Dennis*</u>
Her Husband's Brother
His Wife's Handyman
Her Boyfriend's Back
Her Husband's Boss

<u>*Older Women/Younger Men*</u>
Being Neighborly
Stocking Her Shelves
My Girlfriend's Mother
The Cougar Next Door
Caught by His Neighbor
Cougar on the Hunt

<u>*My Wife, His Submissive*</u>
Stacy Takes a Master
Claiming Her Back Door
Making Her Cuckold Watch
Date Night with Master

<u>*Cheating Wife Stories*</u>
An Eye for Teacher
Taken by the Best Man
Soccer Mom Scores
Taken by Her Ex

About the Author

Avery Rowan has had a titillating fantasy life and, thankfully for us, Avery has decided to share some of those stories with us. Avery's stories contain strong characters, wild adventures, and a high level of steaminess. While each has a happy ending, they also leave you breathing heavy and wishing your lover or battery-operated-boyfriend was near at hand.

Avery lives along the beach in sunny Florida, basking in the sun's rays while the rolling waves provide a soothing white noise to the writing process. When not writing, Avery is with family and friends, getting the most out of this life, just like the characters in Avery's stories. Life is to be lived and savored, not shied away from, so break out of the norms and grab all you can get out of it.

For up-to-date news on Avery's latest releases, book signing events in your area, and giveaways, follow Avery's newsletter - http://eepurl.com/dCBBwP

Also follow Avery at:

Amazon Page ~ https://www.amazon.com/Avery-Rowan/e/B07G7HTBKS

Website ~ http://averyrowan.wordpress.com

Facebook Page ~ https://www.facebook.com/averyrowanauthor/

Made in the USA
Columbia, SC
30 December 2024